By Ethel Calvert Phillips

Cover Design by Phillip Colhouer

Cover Illustration by Anastasiia Khmelevska

Inside Illustrations by Decie Merwin

First published in 1942

© 2019 Jenny Phillips

goodandbeautiful.com

This unabridged version has updated grammar and spelling.

Printed in China

Table of Contents

Brian's Motto 1

The Yankee Clipper 14

Down to Earth 29

On Hickory Drive 40

Lincoln School 54

Chin Up. 65

Rainbow Bridge 78

Here Is Flora 91

The British Benefit. 102

In Place of Victory 113

What They Did 126

Flora's Secret. 137

The Last Day of School 145

To Irene

Chapter One
Brian's Motto

It was spring, and Brian and Mother were alone at Happy-Go-Lucky.

The house seemed strange with only two of them there and not three. Father had always been with them other summers. What fun they had had together, boating on the river and riding and taking long tramps across the moors.

No one could pack a picnic basket quite like Mother. Brian was sure of that. He had learned to row only last summer. Best of all, Brian liked to ride Rob Roy, the brown pony. Rob Roy belonged to Mr. Duff in the village. But Brian was as fond of the shaggy little Shetland as if the pony were his own.

Brian loved it at Happy-Go-Lucky. The very name of the house told you what a carefree, merry life they all led there. You might know that Father

was always thinking of something lively and exciting to do. Mother, her curls tied up with a ribbon, was happy and smiling and full of fun.

But now it was very different. It was wartime in England. Father was far away in Africa with the Army. The village was quiet enough in the daytime, but at night no one except the Home Guard stirred out of doors. Almost every man in the village belonged to the Home Guard. They watched for enemy airplanes and guarded the railway and the bridge. It was so dark you couldn't see where you were going. That was because of the blackout. Every window at Happy-Go-Lucky was covered with black paper. Not a ray of light, not even the flame of a match, must be seen.

There were no more rides on Rob Roy. He was not to be found in Mr. Duff's pasture or stable. Indeed, Mr. Duff himself was gone. He had joined the Royal Air Force. His dogs, too, had vanished. Brian didn't know where.

There was no fuel for the car, so Brian and Mother rode about on bicycles. They rode to the village and into the nearest town. Mother still laughed and made jokes, but somehow it was not the same, and Brian thought he knew why.

"It is because we are listening for the air raid warning," he said to himself. "You never know when it will come. Then, no matter where we are, we have to hurry into the nearest shelter and wait for the All Clear."

Almost everyone had built a shelter behind their house or sometimes in the barn. The shelter at Happy-Go-Lucky was partly in the ground, outside the kitchen door. It was a comfortable shelter with electric lights and shelves and a long wide seat.

The enemy airplanes were bombing the village almost every night. So Mother fixed two beds on the long seat, and there she and Brian slept.

Brian hated the air raids. So did everyone else, for that matter. It was not so much because he was frightened. It was because an air raid always made Mother talk about sending Brian to the United States.

"I started once for America," Brian would say,

"and the ship was torpedoed. I'd much rather stay here with you."

Months before, with a shipload of British evacuated boys and girls, he had sailed for Canada. As he said, their ship had been torpedoed. After four days at sea in a crowded lifeboat, Brian and his companions had been picked up by an English vessel. They had been taken back to port, and Brian had at last reached home.

"You could fly across the ocean this time," Mother always answered. "It would be very different from going on a ship. I should feel much happier if I knew you were safe. Father thinks you ought to go, too."

Brian didn't know how to answer this. He could only hope that the bombings would stop.

But, instead of stopping, the raids came more and more often.

Then, one dreadful night, a bomb fell in a field near Happy-Go-Lucky. Even in the shelter, Brian and Mother could hear terrific noises and one great *Boo-o-om!* when the bomb exploded. Mother held Brian very close.

In the morning, they went to look at the great hole that the bomb had made. The fence was knocked down, too.

It was then that Mother told Brian he was to go to America. She had made up her mind in the night.

"Your papers are ready," said Mother, "and I shall cable Uncle George and Aunt Jane that you are coming."

Uncle George and Aunt Jane Bliss were Father and Mother's friends in the United States. They had written many times asking that Brian come and stay with them until the war was ended.

"I can't go with you," went on Mother, "because Grandpa and Granny are coming here, and they can't manage alone. I shall miss you frightfully. But you will be safe, and perhaps it won't be for long."

Brian meant to be brave about this, but he had to swallow hard before he could speak.

"Perhaps it won't be long," he answered. He even managed to smile back at Mother as he spoke.

"When the war is over, Father and I will come for you, if we can," promised Mother, with a pat on Brian's arm. "Then you can show us all the sights. Now we must both go to work. I want you to start as soon as you can."

In a week, it was all settled. Brian was to fly to Lisbon in Portugal. There he would board a seaplane, the Yankee Clipper, that would carry him over the ocean. Mrs. Russell was going, too, with her baby. She was a neighbor in London where Brian lived in the winter. She would look after Brian, she said.

Now, the day before he was to leave home and England, Brian was riding down the road on his bicycle, his gas mask slung over his shoulder. He was on his way to say goodbye to Mrs. Budge.

Mrs. Budge kept the sweet shop in the village, and she and Brian were good friends.

Past Mr. Duff's house, closed up tight, and past the old gray church, Brian sped.

Here was the Village Green.

The breeze made little ripples chase one another

across the duck pond. But of ducks, white or black, there was not a sign.

"Good! The ducks are hidden away in a safe place," thought Brian.

Mrs. Budge's sweet shop stood on the Green. Brian jumped to the ground before the door.

This was a place he loved to go. He felt at home with Mrs. Budge. He liked the dark little shop that smelled of sweet buns and peppermint.

The shop was really the front room of Mrs. Budge's cottage. It had one large window that held a few jars of sweets. Besides the sweets, Mrs. Budge sold buns and packages of biscuits and vegetables. She had aprons and pins and reels of cotton and stockings for sale, too.

The shop was empty, but Mrs. Budge heard Brian and called to him from the back room.

"Come in, and bring your bicycle," she said. "We will sit down to tea at once, too, just in case."

"In case" meant "in case of an air raid." Brian understood that very well.

The back room was small and crowded with

furniture. No wonder, when it was living room and kitchen in one. You had to pick your way carefully or you might knock over a lamp or an ornament or even stumble into the coal scuttle. Brian, at one time or another, had met with all three of these accidents. But Mrs. Budge was understanding. She said she had been known to do it herself.

The room looked cozy to Brian. He eyed the tea spread out on the table. There were fat sugary buns, bread, plum jam, and a big plate of rock cakes. There was tea for Mrs. Budge and milk for Brian. In wartime, so many good things at once were a very special treat.

Mrs. Budge was plump, with bright black eyes. She smiled across the tea table at the sturdy, sunburned little boy.

There was a great deal to talk about. The moment they sat down, Brian began.

Mrs. Budge was a good listener. Her black eyes snapped with excitement when Brian told all he had heard about flying over the ocean.

"That Yankee Clipper you tell of will be like a bird," cried Mrs. Budge, "like a great seagull flying over the sea."

Brian laughed aloud at this idea.

"I shall be riding on the seagull's back, holding tight with my arms around his neck," he answered. "Only really I shall be inside, looking out of the window all the while."

"Likely there will be other boys and girls with you," went on Mrs. Budge. "And once there, you will find plenty of British children to keep you company. Canada and the States are crowded with them, I've heard."

"I wish I knew where Flora is," said Brian. "Flora MacDonald, I mean. She lives next door to us in London, and we play together. She is Scottish, and she taught me to dance the Highland Fling. Her house is closed up, like ours, and Mother heard she had gone to Canada. But we don't really know."

"You will meet her on the street over there someday, I don't doubt," was Mrs. Budge's hopeful answer. "Now let me show you my Joe's picture. He is in the Navy. Did you know?"

Mrs. Budge took a photograph from the shelf and put it into Brian's hands.

"Twenty years old, Joe is," Mrs. Budge told Brian, "and never gave me a moment's worry, except when he fell into the Vicar's well. And not his fault at that, but a bad boy's mischief, who pushed him in."

Joe was Mrs. Budge's only son. Brian looked at the picture of a dark-eyed young sailor, his smiling face topped by a mop of thick black curls.

"Joe had a motto," said Mrs. Budge with pride. "It was 'Britannia rules the waves.' Joe thought that was a good motto for a sailor."

"So it is," agreed Brian. "It is a song too. Shall I sing it for you?"

"I know it myself," answered Mrs. Budge.

So they sang it together:

"Rule Britannia! Britannia rules the waves!
Britons shall never be slaves."

It was a fine, stirring performance. A neighbor's hen, pecking on the back path, joined in with soft, clucking sounds.

When it was time to go home, Brian and Mrs. Budge shook hands goodbye.

"It was a lovely tea," said Brian. "I will write and tell you about the States and about flying over the ocean."

"Please do," said Mrs. Budge heartily. "And remember, keep smiling. Everything will turn out right."

Brian responded with a thumbs up, then said, "Goodbye, Mrs. Budge. Cherrio!"

All the way home, Brian was thinking of Joe's motto.

"I ought to have a motto, too," he thought.

Mother agreed when Brian told her about it.

"What shall it be?" she said. "Let me think for a moment. I have it! 'Uphold England.' That is a fine motto for a boy who is going to another country."

"So it is."

Brian looked pleased and then thoughtful.

"Uphold England in everything you do and say,"

went on Mother. "You will be showing Americans how English people act and think."

"Uphold England," Brian repeated the words slowly. "That is a good motto, Mother. It is going to be mine."

Chapter Two
The Yankee Clipper

The Yankee Clipper lay at the dock in Lisbon. It was almost time to start on the trip across the ocean. Brian looked at the great silver plane with the American flag painted on her side.

"It is much larger than the plane we came in to Lisbon," thought Brian. "It is the biggest flying boat in the world, I think."

Yesterday, Brian, Mrs. Russell, and her baby had flown to Portugal from a port in England. It was at this English port that Mother and Brian had said goodbye.

"It won't be for long," Mother had said cheerfully.

She had put her arms around Brian and held him tight.

Then, the very last moment, Mother, waving her handkerchief, had called to Brian, "Remember! Uphold England!"

Brian waved back and nodded. Of course he would remember. Why, that was his motto. He couldn't forget.

Now, the last passengers were boarding the Clipper.

Mrs. Russell was going on board. She wore a little scarlet hat tipped down on her smooth black head. A steward was carrying Pamela, the baby, in her Moses basket. The basket was made of reed with a hood. That was the way Pamela traveled. She was only six months old.

Brian started up the gangway. He turned to look at the steep and narrow streets of Lisbon above the harbor. In one of those houses, he and Mrs. Russell and Pamela had slept last night, but which house it was, Brian couldn't tell.

The sky was pink, for the sun was rising. It was daybreak. The Yankee Clipper was making an early start.

"That is because of the wind," thought Brian wisely, "the way a ship has to wait for the tide."

Brian was excited at the thought of the flight before him.

"This morning I am here in Lisbon," he said to himself. "At three o'clock tomorrow afternoon, I shall be in New York."

A steward, trim in his white jacket, was beckoning Brian. He led the way into the compartment where Mrs. Russell sat with Pamela on her lap. There were other people in the compartment. One was a lady, tall and fair, who was bending over a large covered basket. She was talking softly to whatever was inside. Brian wondered what kind of pet it might be.

A door shut. A motor roared. The great seaplane trembled and moved forward. It taxied over the water and then rose into the air.

Brian looked out of the window. The water seemed to be falling away from the plane. He could see more and more of the tumbling green waves. He spied a ship far below.

Now thick white clouds were all about them. Through holes in the clouds beneath, Brian could catch a glimpse of the ocean now and then. They flew higher, and the water was gone.

"It is like flying through cotton wool," Brian thought.

Mrs. Russell and the lady with the basket were talking together. Pamela was taking a nap.

There were sounds from the basket.

"It is a dog," decided Brian. "He is bumping his head against the cover."

He stared so hard at the basket that the lady smiled at him. Her name was Lady Diana Tressidy. She had told Mrs. Russell so.

Mrs. Russell drew Brian forward.

"This is Brian Blythe, Lady Tressidy," she said. "He is going to the United States for the duration to stay with friends."

Brian made a bow. Lady Diana nodded in a friendly way.

"I think Brian might like to see what is in my basket," she said.

She lifted the cover.

There were four cats in the basket, a plump mother cat and three kittens. They were lively kittens. They began to climb over their mother and tumble about.

"Cats!" exclaimed Brian. "Four of them!"

"Yes, four of them," repeated Lady Diana, "and I wouldn't leave one of them behind. The mother is

named Rosanna. She has lived with me so long that I couldn't part with her, and of course the kittens had to come too."

Rosanna was a beautiful snow-white cat. One of the kittens was white like his mother. The other two were gray with white spots. They all had bright green eyes and wise little faces.

Lady Diana lifted the kittens out of the basket, and Brian settled himself comfortably on the floor.

"The gray-and-white kittens are named Spitfire and Hurricane," Lady Diana told him, "because Spitfire spits, and Hurricane rushes madly about."

"They are named for our British fighting planes!" cried Brian. "I know. I have seen both the planes in the air."

"So they are," answered Lady Diana. "But the white kitten has the best name, I think. He is called Victory."

The snow-white kitten acted as if he were proud of his name. He held his ears high. He waved his tail with a lordly air. He was not timid. He walked straight toward Brian and began to box at his hand with soft little paws.

"He is a prizefighter!" cried Brian, delighted. "I like him. Come on, Victory. Come on and win."

He played with the kittens until Bob, the steward, came with lunch. The Yankee Clipper was moving steadily onward. It was a smooth crossing, so far, Bob said.

"I am glad of that," spoke up Brian. "I shouldn't like Victory to be seasick—airsick, I mean."

Victory had no thought of being airsick. He was a good traveler. He looked out of the window with Brian at the fluffy white clouds. The sun was shining on them and made them bright.

Now the plane was flying low. It grew dark. They were passing through a storm. Rain spattered on the windows.

Suddenly Victory spied a white kitten looking in at him through the glass. He sprang forward to meet the stranger—and bumped his nose smartly against the window pane.

Victory looked so surprised that Brian couldn't help laughing.

"That was you, silly," he said. "You saw yourself in the glass."

Victory was angry. Perhaps his feelings were hurt too. No one likes to be laughed at and called "silly."

"S-s-tt!" said Victory, with a cross little spit.

"That bump hurt my nose," was what the spit said.

He jumped down from Brian's lap and walked off with his head and tail high in the air.

There were ten people in the compartment. First, Victory called on a lady who was taking a nap. He woke her by leaping into her lap and knocking her book to the floor.

Then he sat down in front of a man busily reading a newspaper.

"Meow!" called Victory. "Meow!"

The man peered round his paper and saw what it was at his feet.

"Oh, a fellow traveler," said the man pleasantly.

He picked up Victory and rubbed the kitten's soft head.

"Well, well, kitty," he said in a soothing voice. "Flying through the air, aren't you, right over the middle of the Atlantic Ocean? What a wonderful little cat!"

This made Victory feel better.

He jumped down from the man's knee and ran under Bob's feet so suddenly that the steward stepped on the end of Victory's tail.

"Me-e-ow!" cried Victory.

This was too much. His fur stood out, and his eyes looked wild. Victory didn't know which way to run first.

Brian caught him and put him back into his basket. Victory was worn out. He fell asleep.

By this time, Brian was tired of sitting still. He was glad when one of the pilots offered to show him about the Clipper.

The pilot looked like a ship's officer. He wore a blue uniform and a white cap.

On the passenger deck, he showed Brian other compartments where travelers were sitting.

Then he led the way to the upper deck where Brian saw the captain and the officer-pilots. They were busy flying the Clipper. The pilot-navigator and the engineer and the radio officer let Brian watch what they were doing too. It took all seven of them to fly the Clipper.

Downstairs again, on the passenger deck, the pilot handed Brian over to Bob.

"Step into the galley," invited Bob politely, "and look about."

The galley proved to be a neat little kitchen. Brian and Bob sat down to have a talk.

"I suppose you are an American," began Brian. "How do you like having a president instead of a king?"

"It works well," admitted Bob. "It suits me down to the ground."

"I have a book that was given me when I left England," said Brian. "It is called *Token of Freedom*, and it is all about freedom and why the British and the Americans love liberty and believe in it.

There is something in the book that one of your presidents wrote."

"What president was it?" asked Bob.

"Abraham Lincoln," was Brian's answer. "It is about Gettysburg."

Bob looked pleased when he heard this.

"It must be the Gettysburg Address," he told Brian. "I learned it in school. I can say the last part of it now."

He began to recite the fine closing words,

"'... that government of the people, by the people, for the people, shall not perish from the Earth.'"

Brian listened, leaning forward.

"That was splendid," he said when Bob finished. "It sounds like poetry."

"You should learn it," advised Bob. "British or American, it is good to know."

Brian slept that night on the broad seat made into a bed for him by Bob. Pamela slept in her Moses basket. The grown people sat up, with pillows and rugs to make them comfortable.

Before going to bed, Brian said goodnight to Victory. He held the kitten against his face and talked softly into the twitching furry ear.

"I like you best, Vic," whispered Brian. "Spitfire and Hurricane do very well. But I like you best of all."

The next morning, the sun was shining. There were only a few wandering clouds to be seen.

Lady Diana was to leave the plane at Bermuda. Brian was having a last play with Victory. They would have to part before long.

Before they reached Bermuda, Bob pulled down every window shade.

"Bermuda is British, and Britain is at war," explained Bob to Brian. "They don't want outsiders to see what may be going on."

Now the Yankee Clipper was landing. It tipped sharply and then slid onto the water of the harbor.

It was time to say goodbye to Victory. Brian looked around. No one was watching. So Brian kissed Victory quickly, and surprisingly, Victory didn't box back. He put out a rough pink tongue and licked Brian's cheek.

Lady Diana saw all this. She tucked the other kittens into the basket beside their mother. Then she picked up Victory and put him into Brian's arms.

"Two little refugees," said Lady Diana. "Take Victory with you, Brian. Goodbye and good luck."

Then Lady Diana was gone with Rosanna and Spitfire and Hurricane. Brian was left, holding Victory close.

Up rose the Yankee Clipper into the air again. Out of sight of Bermuda, Bob pulled up the shades. This was the last lap of their journey. The trip was nearly at an end.

To Brian, holding Victory, it didn't seem any time at all. Victory belonged to him. Oh, if Mother only knew!

Mrs. Russell smiled at Brian's pleasure. Pamela clapped her hands when Brian put the kitten on her lap. Victory nibbled the toe of her shoe, which made Pamela laugh. Bob brought a box to hold Victory. The lady who had been woken up and the man with the newspaper looked on and smiled. Everyone in the compartment was watching the little boy and his snow-white pet.

"Look, Brian, look at the United States," Mrs. Russell told him. "That is the end of Manhattan Island. That is New York City."

Brian hardly even heard. Victory was yawning. Victory was purring like a grown-up cat. Was there ever so wonderful a pet?

Here was the great airport. Down, down came the Clipper into Bowery Bay. From the flying boat, they boarded a launch that carried them to the dock. They had reached La Guardia Field.

Someone, tall and broad-shouldered and laughing, was calling to Brian. That must be Uncle George. Someone with brown eyes and a smile like Mother was waving her hand. It was Aunt Jane.

"I have come," said Brian, stepping ashore. "Victory and I have come. Here we are in the United States."

Chapter Three
Down to Earth

Uncle George and Aunt Jane acted as if they had always known Brian. He didn't feel at all strange or shy.

Uncle George shook hands with him. This made Brian feel manly and grown-up. Aunt Jane put her arm around his shoulders and pulled him close. That was what Mother often did.

Victory was given a warm welcome. He sat in his box with his head poking out of the hole in the cover. The hole, made by Bob for air, had been quite small. Brian had made it large enough for Victory to put his head through. This was because Brian wanted to see his kitten every single moment. And, of course, Victory wanted to see the world too.

Aunt Jane listened to every word while Brian told all about Victory. She was stroking the kitten's head as he talked.

At last, Aunt Jane spoke.

"I am fond of cats," she said, "but I like kittens even better."

Perhaps Victory felt encouraged by these pleasant words. At any rate, when Uncle George took him out of his box, he climbed up on the shoulder of his new friend. He put out a paw and patted Uncle George's face. He kept his claws tucked in, and when Brian saw that, he felt that everything was going to be all right.

Brian and Mrs. Russell had to go through Customs. They showed their passports and other papers. They had to open their suitcases and bags and let a frowning man with bushy eyebrows look through their belongings. He was a custom house officer, and it was his duty to do this, Uncle George said.

The Customs Officer didn't take long at his task.

"OK," he said, and waved them on.

"OK," repeated Brian under his breath. "That is what they say over here instead of 'righto.' Mother told me they did, and they do."

Now it was Victory's turn. He behaved well. He looked up at the man as if he were not afraid of anyone. He opened his mouth and closed it without making a sound. He waved his tail in the air.

The frowning man smoothed out his bushy eyebrows and even smiled a little.

"He looks healthy," said the Officer. "I think we can safely let him enter the United States."

That was all there was to it. Victory had passed the Customs. There was nothing now to keep them at the airport, so off they all went.

Mrs. Russell's sister had come to meet her, and away drove Mrs. Russell and Pamela. Mrs. Russell made Pamela wave until they were out of sight.

Brian climbed into the front seat of Uncle George's car. Aunt Jane sat in back with Victory.

"Well, here you are in the United States," said Uncle George to Brian. "You flew all the way over the ocean and landed with a white kitten. I don't know any other boy who has done what you have. We must cable your mother and tell her that you are here."

"Tell about Victory, too," put in Brian. "Won't she be surprised?"

They were driving over a great bridge called the Triborough Bridge.

"It connects three of the boroughs of Greater New York," Uncle George told Brian, "the boroughs of Queens, the Bronx, and Manhattan. Soon we shall ride over the two islands. Watch, now, and see."

There was a great deal to look at—the two islands, parks, fine driveways and ships in the river.

Now they were riding through New York City. Brian saw crowds of people. That was like London. But the buildings were taller, and many of them looked new. The air was clear, and the sky was very blue. Everything seemed bright and sparkling. And how strange it was to see the Stars and Stripes flying above the buildings instead of the Union Jack!

Along the broad driveway swept the car. They turned to cross another bridge.

"This is the George Washington Bridge," said Uncle George, "one of the longest bridges in the world. It will take us from New York State into New Jersey where Aunt Jane and I live."

The George Washington Bridge spanned the Hudson River, blue and broad and glittering in the afternoon sun.

"See the Palisades up the river," said Aunt Jane from the back seat, "and then look back at New York."

On the New Jersey shore, the Palisades rose straight out of the water. They were tall steep cliffs of stone. Then Brian looked back at the city of New York with its wonderful skyline of buildings taller than he had ever seen, with the sun shining on turrets and spires and towers.

"You and I will take trips around New York," promised Aunt Jane. "We will go to the Empire State Building and the Bronx Zoo and ever so many places."

Uncle George and Aunt Jane lived in a suburb. It wasn't long before the car carried them through pleasant tree-shaded streets and at last stopped before a white house with a shining knocker on the door. There were trees and bushes about the house and bright yellow daffodils in bloom.

"Here we are," said Uncle George. "Number Seven Hickory Drive. Hop out, Brian. We are home."

"There is Paula, waiting at the door," Aunt Jane said.

Paula was the Polish maid. She was not a smiling person. But she seized Brian's suitcase and carried it upstairs for him. That was Paula's way of welcoming Brian to America.

Then she took Victory from Brian's arms.

"He must have his supper," said Paula. "A big saucer of milk with a dash of cream."

Victory mewed loudly at this good news. He rode off in triumph, looking back at Brian over Paula's wide shoulder.

Aunt Jane helped Brian unpack his bags. But he himself put his photographs of Father and Mother in place on his dresser. He had brought a snapshot of Mrs. Budge standing in her sweet shop door. He was glad to see the three familiar faces in a row.

Then Brian helped Uncle George telephone the cablegram to Mother. First, they wrote it together, and when it was finished, it read like this:

ARRIVED SAFELY HAVE WHITE KITTEN VICTORY WILL WRITE LOVE BRIAN

"That is perfect," said Aunt Jane when she heard it. "Now come to dinner. Brian must be starved."

After dinner, it was not long before Brian was ready to go to bed. Aunt Jane went upstairs with him and tucked him in. Then she sat on the side of the bed to talk.

"There is a boy over the way named Adam," said Aunt Jane. "He has heard all about you, and he has been waiting for you to come. You will like Adam, I am sure."

Before Brian could answer, a doleful sound floated in at the window.

Brian lifted his head.

"Is that a cow?" he asked. "It sounds like a cow with a pain."

The strange, sad sound came again. It died away on a quavering note.

"A cow? No!" said Aunt Jane with a laugh. "That is Adam practicing his clarinet. He hasn't quite learned to play yet. This music is for your benefit, I think. Perhaps it is a lullaby. Goodnight. Sleep well."

There were no more doleful noises. Adam had probably gone to bed. Brian lay very still.

"I am here in the States," he was thinking. "I have flown over the ocean. I am really here."

He heard footsteps, creaking footsteps.

It was Paula coming up the back stairs.

"Asleep?" said Paula in the doorway.

She set a glass of milk and two cookies on the table beside Brian's bed.

"In case you are hungry in the night," said Paula.

"I could eat them now," suggested Brian.

He drank the milk and ate the cookies while Paula watched.

"It is the traveling that makes you hungry," said Paula with a nod. "It is wearing to fly over the ocean. You need food, and tomorrow I shall make little cakes, many of them. Now, goodnight."

A second later, Paula put her head round the doorway.

"The cakes will have icing," said Paula, "and nuts and orange peel."

Then she creaked off downstairs to bed.

In spite of the thought of the little cakes tomorrow, a lump was coming in Brian's throat. He was thinking of Father, far away in Africa. He was thinking about Mother and Happy-Go-Lucky. He wondered what Mother was doing this very minute.

Then he began to wonder who was coming upstairs. He smelled cigar smoke, and he knew.

It was Uncle George. He came in, carrying Victory in the basket Aunt Jane had brought down from the attic for him.

Victory was sitting up straight in the middle of the basket. He looked small and lonely. He opened his mouth and mewed. It was an unhappy little cry.

"Hold your horses, Victory," Uncle George was saying. "Where is the boy who flew over the ocean? Here is another ocean flier, and he needs company. He wants to snuggle up against somebody and go to sleep."

"I'll take him," said Brian eagerly.

He sat up and held out his arms. He was glad to see Victory. It was almost like meeting someone from home.

"I thought you might take him in with you," said Uncle George. "That is why I brought him up."

Brian pushed back the covers, and Victory nestled down beside him. Brian heard him begin to purr. It was a contented, drowsy purr.

Now Victory and Brian were alone. Brian had forgotten the lump in his throat. It was gone.

"We are refugees, both of us," said Brian. "We must Uphold England, don't forget. And there is a boy across the road named Adam. We will like him, Aunt Jane said."

Victory curled himself into a ball. He shut his eyes and went to sleep.

Brian slipped down among the pillows and went to sleep too.

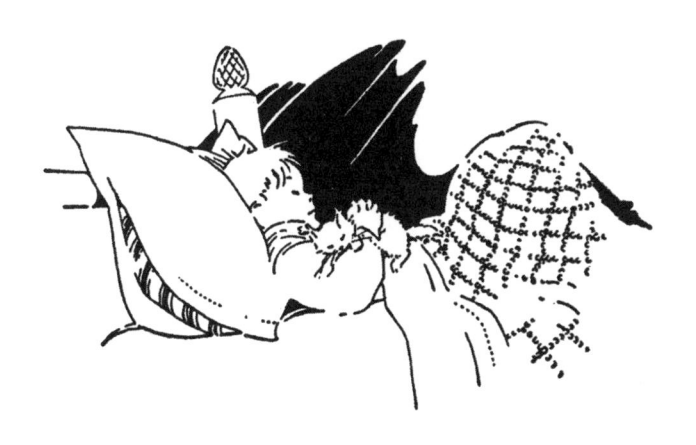

Chapter Four
On Hickory Drive

"Why don't you run over and see Adam?" said Aunt Jane the next morning. "He has been ill and can't come to you. He lives directly across the way."

So Brian started out. He crossed the street and stood looking up at one of the front windows in Adam's house.

A boy was sitting at the window. He wore spectacles and was working at something. Brian could see his hands move.

The boy was Adam. If Brian had only known it, Adam had been watching for a glimpse of the boy from England, but so far with no success.

Now Adam spied Brian standing on the lawn. He pounded on the window, smiling broadly. He beckoned to Brian. He held up two fingers and made the V for Victory. He opened his mouth and seemed to be calling. The window was closed, and Brian couldn't hear what he said.

But Adam's mother must have heard him. The front door opened, and Mrs. Monroe came out on the steps.

"You are Brian Blythe, aren't you?" said she pleasantly. "You see, I know your name. Come upstairs. Adam can't wait to meet you."

Adam began to call out before Brian was in the room.

"Hello," he cried. "I thought you would never come. I want to hear all about the Clipper. Do you think you will like it in America? Sit down here, right by me."

Adam was sitting in an armchair with a stool under his feet and a rug across his knees. The room was filled with sunshine. In one corner stood an aquarium, and on the floor was a box in which a small turtle, named Poke, was trying to climb up the sides.

Adam was a round-faced boy with a cheerful smile. His spectacles gave him a wise look. His arms were thin and his neck was not much bigger than a pipestem, but this was because he had been ill.

"Adam has had pneumonia," said his mother. "But he is almost well now. Before long, he will be going to school again. Perhaps you two will be in the same class."

The doorbell rang, and Mrs. Monroe went downstairs to answer it.

"Tell me about the trip," began Adam. "Tell me everything. How did you feel when you were flying so high with nothing but the ocean underneath?"

"I liked it," said Brian. "It wasn't scary. I brought a white kitten with me. He is English too. He was given to me on the Clipper, and his name is Victory."

"A refugee kitten!" exclaimed Adam. "I have never seen one. Bring him over this afternoon, will you? Victory is a good name. I am doing my bit to help you win. I am knitting socks for your soldiers. Look!"

Adam held up a strange gray object. It was very long and very narrow. Brian thought it looked more like a belt or a necktie than a sock. But of course he didn't say so.

"My father is a Captain in the British Army," he told Adam. "He is in Africa."

"He may have my socks," said generous Adam promptly. "You could send them to him. They might save him from frostbite."

Brian shook his head.

"They wouldn't fit him," he answered. "Nobody in the British Army has legs as thin as that. That sock looks as if it might fit a giraffe."

The thought of a giraffe in army socks made the boys laugh.

"He could wear a helmet, too, with his ears sticking out," added Brian, "and a scarf."

This was so funny that Adam beat upon the window sill and rocked to and fro.

"Did you hear me playing a salute to you last night?" asked Adam, when he had recovered from his laughing spell. "It was meant to be 'Yankee Doodle.' But Mother said it was just a terrible noise."

"Aunt Jane told me it was you playing," said Brian. "I had gone to bed."

"My Aunt Lou sent me the clarinet because I was sick," explained Adam, "but I don't play it very well yet. The tune never comes out the way I think it will. Now tell me more about the Clipper and about your father in Africa. I suppose there is lots of sand and camels humping around. Does your father fight with tanks? Have you ever been in one?"

The morning went by quickly. Brian told of his flight in the Yankee Clipper and how Victory now belonged to him. He told of Rob Roy and boating on the river and picnics in the woods. Adam listened eagerly. His knitting fell to the floor.

When Brian told of sailing for Canada and how the ship had been torpedoed, Adam stared at him with admiring eyes.

Brian's Victory

"Gee, are you brave!" said Adam. "You will get along all right in school here. Anyway, I will be there in a couple of weeks to show you around. Do you keep a stamp book? Maybe we can trade. I'd like a stamp from Africa."

Brian went home happy and excited.

"Adam is just like the boys at school," he told Aunt Jane. "He talks a little different, but that doesn't matter. He wants to see Victory this afternoon."

The kitchen was sweet with the odor of baking. Paula had been making little cakes, as she had promised. Brian ate three. They tasted just as good as they had sounded the evening before.

In the afternoon, Aunt Jane went off to a meeting of her Garden Club. Paula creaked upstairs to her room to rest.

"Now is the time to take Victory over to see Adam," thought Brian.

But first he helped himself to a few more cakes.

There was no one to say a word, but Brian felt he should explain what he was doing.

"Paula would want me to eat them," said he.

When the cakes had vanished, he looked for his cat.

But where was Victory?

He was not in his basket. He was not lying in the sun on the back porch.

At last Brian found him at the end of the garden. He was prowling through the grass, like a little tiger, on some errand of his own.

When Brian tried to catch Victory, off went the kitten with a wild leap. He scampered in and out among the bushes and then dashed boldly into the next garden.

Brian followed. There was nothing else for him to do.

The gray stucco house in the garden was long and low. On the side grew a wisteria vine, heavy with purple blossoms.

A French window stood wide open. Over the lawn and in at the window went Victory. Brian was close behind.

It was a large room that Victory had entered.

A young man was sitting at a desk. He was writing so busily that he didn't know Victory was there until he felt the kitten's sharp claws on his ankle. Victory was trying to climb up the young man's leg.

The man dropped his pen and peered down at his feet in surprise.

"I say, what's all this?" he exclaimed. "A kitten! Where did you come from?"

He picked up Victory and stood him on his desk.

Victory was just as startled as the man had been. His green eyes gleamed. His fur stood out. He looked almost round, like a ball.

"He is my kitten, Victory," spoke up Brian from the window. "He ran away from me. I have come to live next door. I am Brian Blythe."

"Oh, I know who you are," said the young man with a nod. "You are just over from England, aren't you?"

He stood up, and Brian saw that he was straight and tall.

"My name is John Van Dusen," he was saying.

"You may call me Van, if you like, because everyone does."

Van had a friendly look that made Brian feel as if he had known him for years. There was a twinkle in his eye, too, and Brian knew at once that he was going to like Van.

"You English are a brave people," said Van. "How was the bombing when you left home? I have been over there and seen it. I write for papers and the magazines."

A sound came from the desk. It was a loud, imperious mew. Victory didn't mean to be forgotten. His ears were standing up straight. His tail was waving in a most lordly fashion.

Van sat down at his desk and took Victory into his hands.

"Come now, kitten," he said. "You have just scratched my ankle and never said 'Excuse me.' Don't put on airs with me. You act as if you were royalty."

And Van raised his eyebrows at Victory in a comical way that made Brian laugh.

"He belonged to Lady Diana Tressidy," said Brian. "She was traveling on our Clipper, and she gave him to me."

"There! Didn't I tell you? I felt it in my bones," said Van with a sober face. "A Lady is almost royalty, isn't she? Probably Victory's grandmother is catching mice this minute in Buckingham Palace."

Brian laughed again. But he couldn't help wondering whether this might not be true. Victory was not an ordinary kitten. Perhaps he was related to a royal cat.

"How would you like a ride?" Van asked Brian. "I have an errand at the Post Office. You whip home with Victory while I type my letter. Then I will be ready to start."

Brian was back so soon that Van was still clacking away at the typewriter. So the little boy walked slowly about the big room. It was Van's library, he decided. The walls were lined with books. There was a globe of the world so large that

Brian's arms wouldn't reach around it. He whirled the globe until he found Africa. He put his finger on the very spot where he thought Father might be.

He showed this place to Van when the letter was finished. He told Van about Father and Mother and Happy-Go-Lucky as they rolled down the hill in Van's car. He even told about his motto, "Uphold England," because he knew that Van would understand.

Then Brian heard about Van's trip to England. What a pity he had not traveled on the Yankee Clipper, for that meant he had never met Bob.

Brian learned that Van lived all alone in the gray stucco house with a manservant named Logan.

"He does all the work," said Van. "Logan is my Paula."

Van made up a game as they drove along. It happened to be about his car, but they could play it about anything at all, he said.

"English and American people use different words for the same thing," explained Van. "I will call out an American word, and you must give the English one. Or, if you call out, I must answer. But it must be done as quick as a snap."

Brian understood. "Righto," he said.

"OK," answered Van. "That is a good start."

This was going to be fun.

"Windshield," began Van.

"Windscreen," said Brian. And he was right.

"Hood," said Van next.

"Bonnet," answered Brian.

"Muffler," called Van quickly.

"Silencer," cried Brian.

The next ones weren't so easy.

"But it is simple when you know it," said Brian at last. "Your bumper is our fender, and our dicky seat is your rumble."

"I think you deserve an ice cream soda after that," said Van. "Have you ever had one?"

Brian shook his head.

So they went to the Drug Store, which at home Brian would have call the Chemist's, and there, seated on a high stool, he tasted his first ice cream soda.

"You might begin with a Black-and-White," suggested Van.

This had a mysterious sound. Brian was eager to know what it was. It proved to be a chocolate soda with vanilla ice cream.

"It is good," said Brian when there wasn't a drop left in his glass. "I like it better than Mrs. Budge's ginger beer."

Then they took a turn out into the country. The spring wind blew in Brian's face. The dogwood was in blossom. The sky was a deep clear blue.

When Brian reached home, it was too late to take Victory over to see Adam. So Brian sat down on the front steps to watch for Uncle George.

Suddenly, Adam appeared in his window. He beckoned hurriedly. He raised the window without a sound. It was plain that he didn't want someone to know he was there.

"My Aunt Lou has come to dinner," called Adam in a loud whisper. "She has brought me another present. It is an airplane builder. She heard me play

'Yankee Doodle,' and she says I have to wait and grow up to the clarinet. Mother is glad of it. See you tomorrow."

Adam vanished. His mother took his place. She closed the window sharply.

Uncle George was walking up the street from the train, and Brian ran to meet him. Uncle George would want to hear all about Brian's day.

Chapter Five
Lincoln School

Lincoln School was a large new brick building.

"It doesn't look at all like Homewood," thought Brian, as he and Aunt Jane walked up the front steps.

Homewood was the boarding school in England where Brian had gone until he started for Canada. The school was closed now because most of the boys had been sent away from England or had gone where it was thought to be more safe. The

Masters were serving in the Army or the Navy. Even old Doctor Colton, the Headmaster, was now a member of the Home Guard.

Homewood was a rambling wooden building with lattice windows and turrets and many gables. Brian was right. The two schools did not look at all alike.

Aunt Jane led the way down a broad hall to the Principal's Office. Doctor Flower was the name of the Principal. He and Aunt Jane knew one another.

Doctor Flower asked Brian a few questions about his studies in England.

"You belong in the Fifth Grade," he decided. "I will take you to the classroom myself."

"We say Form, not Grade," thought Brian, remembering Van's game.

He didn't mean to tell this to Doctor Flower, but if he had, there would not have been time. He could hardly say goodbye to Aunt Jane because everything was done in such a hurry. Doctor Flower was a large, stout man, but he was as light on his feet as a rubber ball. He walked so quickly that Brian almost had to run to keep up.

Doctor Flower threw open the door of a classroom. The room was filled with boys and girls.

"We didn't have girls at Homewood," thought Brian. "But I don't mind. Flora was lots of fun."

The boys and girls were sitting at tables, two by two. They were busy, but everyone stopped work and looked up when Brian entered the room.

The Principal didn't seem to mind this, and neither did the teacher. Her name was Mrs. King. She was small, and her voice was quiet. But Brian soon learned that the class listened when Mrs. King spoke.

Brian was seated at a table beside a boy named Louis Ferrara. Louis had black eyes and black hair and brown skin. He smiled in a friendly way every time that Brian looked at him.

What Brian noticed first of all in the classroom were the large windows. The sun came pouring into the room. He liked the pictures hanging above the blackboards. There was the picture of a pony that looked like Rob Roy, except that he was not a Shetland, and another picture of two boys fishing on the banks of a stream.

Before Brian could turn and look at the other pictures, an electric bell sounded. The noise made Brian jump, for at first he thought it was an air raid warning. But that was only for a second. He saw that the bell meant it was time for school to begin.

Mrs. King called the roll, and Brian listened. At Homewood, all the boys were British, but here the members of his class seemed to have come from almost every nation of the world.

"Louis Ferrara is an Italian name, and Margaretta Blum is German," thought Brian. "Michael Murphy is Irish."

That was as far as Brian could go.

He didn't know that sturdy little Barbara Novak's father and mother had come from Hungary and Trinidad Castro's parents from South America and Stanley Koshenski's people from Poland.

But, whatever the nation might be, Brian was soon to learn that these children with foreign names were good Americans, loyal to the United States and to the American flag.

Once the roll was called, Brian was kept busy. Lessons in arithmetic, spelling, geography, and history followed one after the other. Brian went home at noon with an armful of books.

"There is homework," cried Brian rushing in upon Aunt Jane. "We have penmanship too. We never had penmanship at Homewood. Two boys in my class walked home with me. They know Adam. Their names are Charles Robinson and Walter Collins."

"Is Adam in your class too?" asked Aunt Jane.

"Yes, he is," answered Brian. "Mrs. King, my teacher, told me so. I say, I like Mrs. King. She is lots more friendly than old Squibby ever was."

"Squibby?" repeated Aunt Jane. "Who is he?"

"Mr. Squibbs, my room teacher at Homewood," explained Brian. "He never laughed. He always looked like this." And naughty Brian made a gloomy face, at which Aunt Jane didn't smile at all.

This sent Brian off in a hurry to wash his hands without being told.

Before Brian went back to school, he stepped into the kitchen to say goodbye to Victory.

"There is going to be an Assembly this afternoon," he told Paula. "No more lessons today. I think school is going to be easier here than it is at home."

In the classroom again, Brian didn't jump when the electric bell sounded. He was used to it now.

The bell told that it was time for Assembly, and downstairs went the children.

In the large Assembly Room, Brian found himself standing between Charles Robinson and Walter Collins in one of the long rows of seats. They were facing a platform on which stood Doctor Flower. The other classes were filing in. Soon every seat was filled.

On the platform was a fine American flag.

Suddenly, every hand in the room, except Brian's, snapped to attention.

They were giving the Salute to the Flag.

"'I pledge allegiance to the flag of the United States of America,'" they began.

The whole school recited steadily as one person. They were not foreigners, Hungarians, Poles, Italians, Germans. They were Americans, every one.

"'. . . one nation, under God, indivisible, with liberty and justice for all.'"

That was the end. The school sat down.

Doctor Flower rose and began to talk to the children. He spoke of starting early for school and not being late.

Brian's eyes wandered and he noticed words painted on the wall beside the platform.

He read them:

That government of the people, by the people, for the people, shall not perish from the Earth. Abraham Lincoln.

The words were familiar. Brian had heard and read them before.

"Bob said that to me on the Clipper," Brian remembered. "It is about Gettysburg. It is in my book, *Token of Freedom*, too. 'That government of the people, by the people. . .'"

Brian was reading the words again when Walter Collins gave his arm a nudge.

Doctor Flower was still talking.

". . . an English boy," Doctor Flower was saying, "who has come to America and is now a pupil in Lincoln School."

Brian sat up.

"Does he mean me?" he wondered.

"His name is Brian Blythe," went on Doctor Flower, "and we should like to have him step up on the platform and tell you boys and girls some of his experiences coming over here."

"Oh, I can't," thought Brian. "I won't."

It wasn't easy for Brian to speak before people. When his teacher, Mr. Squibbs, had insisted that

Brian recite at a Homewood entertainment, Brian had been miserable for days before and very happy when it was over.

"I can't," he said to himself again, "and I won't."

But, strangely enough, at the same time he was thinking this, he was standing and walking toward the platform. This was because, in the back of his mind, he was repeating two words over and over. The two words were "Uphold England."

That was his motto, and this was his first chance to Uphold England in the United States. No matter what happened, Brian didn't mean to fail.

Brian mounted the platform. If his teeth were shut very tight, no one knew it but he.

It wasn't so hard after all. Brian told just what had happened.

"I lived in London," said Brian. "And when London was bombed, I got on a ship with other British boys and girls to go to Canada. The ship was torpedoed, and we stood on the deck with the water over our ankles. I was put in a lifeboat, but, halfway down, the boat stuck, and a sailor cut the rope with his knife. The boat fell into the water, but it landed right side up. We were three days at sea with only ship's biscuits to eat. But we were picked up by an English vessel and taken to Liverpool. I was sent home, and after a while I flew to Lisbon and came here on the Yankee Clipper."

It was over. Brian started to walk off the platform, but he was taken aback by the burst of applause from the whole school. The children understood very well that this was a story of heroism told in a modest, simple way. They all clapped for Brian as hard as they could. Doctor Flower and the teachers were applauding too.

Brian's cheeks burned. He was glad to slip into his seat again between Walker and Charles.

Charles, smiling broadly, slapped Brian's knee.

"That was swell," he whispered. "Come round someday, and see my white mice."

Walter nudged Brian's arm again with a friendly elbow and slipped a sticky Lifesaver into his hand.

It was their way of telling Brian that they were proud of him and liked him too.

Brian felt very happy. He had upheld England, as Mother had wished him to do, and here in America, after only a few days, he was not a stranger. He was among friends.

Chapter Six
Chin Up

The whole day had gone wrong for Brian.

It began in the morning when he and Adam were running to school. They thought they were late. Adam had overslept. Brian was behind time because he couldn't fasten his snake belt. The clasp wouldn't stay shut.

Brian was proud of his snake belt. All the boys in his school in England had worn one. It was a leather belt with a buckle in the form of a snake, neatly coiled.

"I don't believe anyone in the United States has a snake belt like mine," Brian often thought.

Then he would give the snake an affectionate pat.

But this morning, there was no time for patting. Brian had to run downstairs to breakfast. Aunt Jane had called him twice.

Brian and Adam hurried along as fast as they could. Adam was well now. He and Brian sat at the same table in their classroom. Louis Ferrara hadn't minded changing his place at all.

The trouble began when Adam laughed at Brian. He laughed because Brian told him that Victory was a royal cat.

Brian almost believed that this was true about his kitten. The truth was, he wanted to believe that this was so. He could picture Victory's grandmother prowling about Buckingham Palace and pouncing swiftly upon any unwary mouse. And if such a grandmother, living in a palace with the King, the Queen, and the two Princesses, didn't make Victory royal, what would? Brian chose to forget that this was only an imaginary grandmother, invented by Van for a joke. Anyway, Adam shouldn't have laughed so rudely, Brian thought.

"A royal cat!" exclaimed Adam, slapping his leg as he laughed. "Who ever heard of such a thing? We don't have royal cats or even royal people over here. We don't think anything of them at all."

"Oh, don't you?" answered Brian quickly. "Then why did you and your mother stand for hours in New York to see our King and Queen ride by, when they were here on a visit? You told me you did that yourself."

"I wanted to see them as a curiosity," said Adam.

At this speech, Brian's face grew red. He doubled up his fists. He wanted to fight Adam. But he didn't have a chance, for already Adam was running off to tell Charles and Walter and Stanley what Brian had said.

Out of the corner of his eye, Brian could see them all laughing. This made him stiff his back. They were not late, after all. But Brian marched off to his classroom alone. He didn't want to talk to the boys. He told himself he would never speak to Adam again.

"Chin up," he thought. "I shan't let these American boys see that I care what they say."

In spite of this firm resolve, Brian couldn't help thinking of what had happened.

"Why shouldn't I have a royal cat?" he asked himself over and over. "Adam doesn't know everything in the world."

Brian spent quite a little time keeping Adam over on his own side of the table. He spread out his elbows and pushed whenever Adam came too near.

He found it hard to put his mind on his work. That may have been why Brian failed in his history lesson. And he couldn't do his problems in arithmetic, no matter how much he figured and rubbed out.

"This is the meanest day I have ever lived through," thought Brian when the bell rang at five minutes til twelve, and he was free to rush home to lunch.

But Brian had not lived through the day yet. Something worse was to happen.

The moment Paula saw him in the kitchen door she asked, "Where is your belt?"

The snake belt was gone. No feeling around his waist nor peering down would bring it back.

This was too much. Brian shut his teeth tight and stamped his foot.

"That won't help you," said Paula. "If your Aunt Jane was home, she would find it for you. She is a good looker. But she has gone to a big luncheon of the Garden Club."

Brian didn't answer. Without a word, he turned around and hurried back to school the way he had come home. He searched carefully all along the way, but there was no belt to be seen anywhere. It was only three blocks to school, but they seemed very long ones. Brian was hot and tired and hungry when at last he came back home without his belt.

Paula was good to him. She knew how much Brian thought of his belt.

"You will find it yet," said Paula.

"Maybe you lost it at school."

This was encouraging. Perhaps he had. Brian hadn't thought of that.

"You are already going to be late getting back," said Paula, "so take your time, and don't eat so fast. Ask your teacher to let you hunt for your belt in the school the very first thing."

This was good advice, and Brian followed it.

Mrs. King was sorry about the loss of the belt.

Adam made friends at once, when he heard of it.

"Gee, that is too bad," he said.

He hunted in the cloakroom and poked in cupboards and corners looking for the belt, but with no success.

Mrs. King let Brian take a note to every classroom, asking if anyone had seen the snake belt.

But no one had seen it. The belt was lost.

The afternoon dragged on. It seemed endless.

"I wish it was time to go home," Brian kept thinking. "I am glad it is Friday."

The hands of the clock crept slowly around. Only ten minutes more! Work was put away. The tables were cleared. The room was set in order.

Mrs. King was standing before the class.

"I want each one of you to learn a poem," she was saying, "and be prepared to recite it one week from today. Choose whatever you like, but tell me your choice on Monday. Perhaps someone from this class will be chosen to recite at the entertainment on the last day of school. The class is dismissed."

Out in the hall, Brian made a dreadful face.

"Mrs King is just like Squibby," he was thinking. "She isn't a bit better. I don't like poems. I don't want to recite. I don't like anything now that my snake belt is gone."

Adam drove off to the dentist with his mother. Brian went home alone.

"Aunt Jane is out," thought Brian. "I'll go see Van, if the sign isn't there."

The sign said, in large letters, DO NOT DISTURB. If it hung on the French window, it told Brian that Van was too busy for callers.

But this afternoon there was no sign. Van

wasn't working at his desk. He was reading in a comfortable chair.

"Radio," said Van when Brian appeared.

"Wireless," answered Brian.

They were still playing the game about English and American words. It was a game that seemed to have no end.

"Phonograph," said Van next.

"Gramophone," said Brian.

But his face was so sober that Van put down his book.

"What is the matter, old chap?" he asked. "Is it something you can tell me?"

Indeed it was. Brian was glad to tell it all—the loss of the snake belt, Adam laughing at the royal cat, and then about learning a poem.

"I can't learn a poem," said Brian dolefully. "It seems as if I could jump off a bridge sooner than do that."

Van looked thoughtful. "No matter how bad things are," he said, "you usually can do something to make them better. Don't you suppose your mother could buy you another snake belt?"

"Perhaps she could," said Brian doubtfully. "I can write and ask her, I suppose."

"Now about the royal cat," Van went on. "Hadn't you better laugh with Adam about that? We weren't talking about pedigrees, you know. It was all a joke."

Brian felt a little more cheerful. It seemed different when Van put it that way.

"Righto," he said. "I don't really care about the cat. But I can't learn a poem, Van. There is no way around that."

"What is the matter with poetry?" asked Van. "I like it. Why don't you?"

"It isn't the poetry," said Brian. "It is because I don't know what to choose, and I don't like to recite anyway. I wouldn't mind if I could learn what Bob said to me. It is on the wall of our Assembly Room at school."

"What is that?" asked Van.

"'That government of the people, for the people, by the people shall not perish from the Earth,'" repeated Brian. "It sounds like poetry, even if it isn't. I think it is great."

"So do I," agreed Van. "That is one of the finest pieces of writing in the English language. Do you know what it is?"

"Lincoln's Gettysburg Address," answered Brian. "It is in my *Token of Freedom*, the book they gave me when I left England. I should like to learn that."

"Then learn it," advised Van. "Unless your teacher insists on a poem, she will be pleased."

"I will go home," said Brian, "and get my book."

What a help Van had been! It was the way Mother made things come out right.

When Brian came running back, his face was beaming. He rushed into the room, waving both arms. In one hand he flourished a small book. That was to be expected. But from the other hand dangled a belt!

"Look! Look!" cried Brian. "My belt! It is found! See! Look!"

It was the snake belt. You couldn't mistake it.

"Aha!" said Van, laughing. "Safe in your bureau drawer all the while, I suppose." He raised his eyebrows and gave Brian a comical look.

"Of course not!" exclaimed Brian. "I did lose it. I lost it on the way to school. Miss Birch was in her window and saw it fall off."

Miss Birch was a little old lady, a friend of Aunt Jane. Van knew her too. She was quite deaf, and because she lived alone, she often sat by the window to see people pass by.

"Why didn't Miss Birch call out and tell you about your belt?" asked Van. "Then you wouldn't have had such a run-around."

"She says that she did knock on the window," said Brian, "but I didn't hear her. So she took my belt to the Garden Club luncheon and gave it to Aunt Jane. Aunt Jane just brought it home."

"Good," said Van. "Hand it over."

With his big library shears, he straightened and tightened the clasp.

"There! Your belt won't fall off again when you're in a hurry," he said. "Now let me see your book."

The *Token of Freedom* was a small, cream colored book with palm and laurel leaves on the cover. There were figures, too, which Brian explained to Van.

"That woman is Britannia saying goodbye to a boy," he said, "and the other is America welcoming a girl. Inside, it tells what great people have said about freedom and patriotism and things like that."

Van read the words printed on the cover. Brian's name had been written in ink in the proper place.

> This Token of Freedom
> Was given to me
> Brian Blythe
> When I was 10 years old
> By someone who loved these words
> And knew what they meant
> And knew why I must cherish them
> And hold them sacred
> So long as I live.

Van read the words carefully.

"Splendid," he said, when he came to the end.

"Take good care of this book. The older you grow, the more you will prize it."

"Here is what Lincoln said," and Brian turned the leaves hastily until he found the page.

"Abraham Lincoln," read Brian. "This is what he said in dedicating the battlefield of Gettysburg during the American Civil War.

"'Forescore and seven years ago...'"

"I can learn that," said Brian, interrupting himself. "I want to learn it, every word. You know my motto, Van. Don't you think I will be upholding England if I learn to say this?"

"There is no question about it," answered Van. "You couldn't do better."

"I know what to learn, and my belt is found," said Brian happily, giving the snake belt a pat. "I thought this was a dreadful day, but it has turned out well, after all."

Chapter Seven
Rainbow Bridge

It was Sunday afternoon, and Brian and Uncle George and Aunt Jane were riding uptown in New York City on a big Fifth Avenue bus. They had climbed a tiny stairway to the seats on top so that Brian might see the buildings and the long line of the great Avenue that stretched ahead.

Brian's cheeks were red with excitement. Every now and then, he whistled softly to himself. It was what Brian always did when he felt very happy. If Mother had been there, she could have told you so.

It was not the fine shops nor the huge city nor the merry scene that made Brian so happy. It was because something wonderful was to happen that very afternoon.

Brian was going to talk to Mother in London, and Mother was going to talk to him!

All this was to happen on a short wave broadcast of British refugee children to their parents in England. The name of the broadcast was Rainbow Bridge.

Brian liked the name the moment he heard it.

"When Mother and I talk together," he said, "it will be just as if we walked over a rainbow bridge and met one another."

"So it will," agreed Aunt Jane, "a great rainbow of promise stretching between England and America. It is a promise of loyalty and friendship between the two countries."

Brian nodded.

"It means that we stand together," he said.

Brian was thinking of all this as he rode along.

At Rockefeller Center, Uncle George stopped the bus. Brian was used to the buses in London. He didn't mind how much the bus swayed and jolted, nor how steep and narrow the stairway might be.

"Look at the British Empire Building," said Aunt Jane as they crossed the street.

She pointed out to Brian the British coat of arms carved above the beautiful door and, at the sight of it, Brian straightened with pride.

They walked along the Promenade and through the Sunken Plaza, where people were eating outside at small tables under bright umbrellas.

A huge fountain was playing here. It was called the Prometheus Fountain. It showed the figure of a man holding aloft a golden flame. All about the edge of the fountain walked plump little penguins.

"They come from the Bronx Zoo," said Aunt Jane, as they stopped to watch the droll little fellows waddle about. "They did have sea lions in the fountain. But one of them came out and climbed into a lady's lap. So they took them away and brought the penguins instead."

The tall building from which Brian was to broadcast loomed before them.

"Only seventy stories high," said Uncle George cheerfully. "How would you like to walk to the top?"

But instead of walking, they shot up in an elevator and were shown into a room where Brian took his place at a table with eight other boys and girls. They were different ages and sizes, but all were British and all were happy at the thought of talking with Mother and Father at home.

A pleasant man was in charge. His name was Ben Bower. He made everyone, even the shyest, feel comfortable by his easy manner and his nods and smiles.

Only the children sat in the studio with Ben Bower. Uncle George and Aunt Jane, with the other grown people, were seated in the gallery behind a glass screen. But they could hear perfectly because of the loudspeaker that brought them every word.

The children sat waiting. Each one wore a pair of earphones. A big shiny microphone stood on the table. On the wall, a clock with a clear white face measured off the seconds.

"Mother is waiting for me in London," thought Brian. "She is sitting in a studio too. But it is dark over there. It is night in England."

At exactly two-thirty, Ben Bower began talking into the microphone. He spoke as softly as if he were talking to someone in the room and not to people who were three thousand miles away. That was the way the children had been told to talk, too.

"This is Rainbow Bridge," said Ben Bower. "These are British children in New York and Canada greeting their parents in England. They are sitting in the studio wearing earphones, and they all look very happy and expectant. Today they are to talk to parents in London, Manchester, and Newcastle."

"Are you ready, Canada? Are you ready, Bill Ward? Good, Canada is ready."

"Hello, B.B.C. This is New York calling. Come in, B.B.C.?"

"Hello, New York, hello," came the voice from England.

"Well, now we are off," said Ben Bower. "Here are three children: John, Michael, and Patricia West. They are five, seven, and nine years old. Are you there, Mrs. West? Patricia is bursting to talk to you. We will let her begin."

"Don't let her burst," said Mrs. West with a laugh. "How are you, Patricia? Tell me what you have been doing lately. Have you any special news?"

Patricia told the news that she was taking music lessons and had been to the Bronx Zoo.

Michael told that he had three new teeth and had gained five pounds.

"He looks very well and plump, Mrs. West," said Ben Bower, "and he has a wide and gaping smile. Now here is John."

The small five-year-old boy was seated on the table in front of the microphone.

"Hello, Johnny darling," said his mother. "Are you wearing your soldier suit?"

Johnny couldn't answer.

"Don't be afraid of the microphone," said Ben Bower, laughing. "Speak up, and say 'Yes.'"

So Johnny spoke up bravely.

"Yes, Mommy," he said, "and I go to play school now."

"What a big boy!" said his mother. "Your dog, Princie, sends all three of you a terrific tail wag, and your aunts and uncles and cousins and friends send their love. Goodbye."

"Say goodbye," said Ben Bower.

And the three little Wests, one by one, called goodbye.

"Brian Blythe is next," said Ben Bower.

Brian didn't mean to lose a moment. He began talking at once.

"Hello, Mother, this is Brian," he began. "How are you and everybody and is Happy-Go-Lucky safe?"

"I am very well, Brian," said Mother's familiar voice.

How glad Brian was to hear it again.

"Happy-Go-Lucky is just as you left it," went on Mother. "We have not been bombed lately, you know. Grandpa and Granny send their love. Grandpa is a Fire Warden, and Granny is knitting a pullover for you. Did you get my last letter about Rob Roy?"

"No, I have not yet," answered Brian. "What about Rob Roy?"

"Only that Mr. Duff has been home on leave," answered Mother, "and tells me that Rob Roy is in a very safe place. He says that you will be riding him again as soon as the war is over."

"That's topping," said Brian. "How is Mrs. Budge?"

"She is well," said Mother, "and wishes you were here to eat some of her sweet buns."

"Please thank her for me," said Brian politely. "I have had two letters from Father, and Uncle George and Aunt Jane are here with me and send their love. Give my love to Granny and Grandpa, and write to me soon, Mother."

"I will, Brian," said Mother. "Remember, Uphold England. Goodbye."

It was someone else's turn now. Brian didn't notice what was going on about him. He was thinking over every word that Mother had said. She had sounded so near. It was almost as if she were here in the room.

After a little, Brian began to listen again.

Bill Ward in Canada was speaking, and this is what he said:

"Flora MacDonald in Montreal, Canada, will talk now with her parents in Newcastle, England."

Flora MacDonald! That was the name of Brian's

friend and playmate in London. Could there be two Flora MacDonalds? Suppose this should be his friend!

"Hello, Mommy," a little girl's voice was saying. "It is so good to hear you speak. Your birthday present came in time. Thank you very much. I love my silver bracelet. It is the most beautiful bracelet in the world. I am wearing it now."

It was Flora's voice. Brian knew it at once. Flora always talked with a bit of a Scottish burr. And how like her to love her new bracelet and think it the most beautiful one in the world.

Brian longed to speak to her. If he didn't speak up now, he might never find her again. But he knew he mustn't interrupt the broadcast. If he could only whisper to Ben Bower and tell him how it was. But Ben was busy. His eyes were fixed on the clock.

Flora was still talking.

"Hello, Daddy," she was saying now. "I have grown three inches, and I have a fine new plaid dress that Auntie Grace made for me. It is the MacDonald plaid, our Clan tartan. Auntie Grace said you would surely like to hear about it."

"I am glad you told me," said Mr. MacDonald. "I want to see that dress. I am coming to bring you home when the war is over, and mind you don't wear your dress out before we meet."

Flora was gone now. A little boy from Vancouver told his mother about a forest fire he had seen, and two sisters in Toronto talked with their parents in Manchester. The other children in the studio with Brian each had a turn too.

Then the time was up.

"Good afternoon, Canada. Goodnight, England," said Ben Bower. "This is the National Broadcasting Company."

The broadcast was over.

Parents and friends were coming down from the gallery. Everyone looked excited and pleased.

Brian could hardly wait to see Uncle George and Aunt Jane.

"Did you hear Mother?" he exclaimed. "She

sent her love to you both. I am going to ride Rob Roy again. And Flora is here in America. Flora MacDonald. I have told you about her. She spoke on the broadcast. She is in Montreal."

Brian couldn't stop talking. He went from Flora to Mother and back to Flora again.

"Couldn't I write to her?" he begged. "Can't we find out where she is in Montreal?"

Uncle George thought they could. He asked Ben Bower.

"Certainly," said Ben Bower. "The Broadcasting Station in Canada will have her address. Sit tight, young man. You will hear from me in a day or so."

This had been a glorious and exciting day. Brian sat between Uncle George and Aunt Jane in the open-air restaurant and ate ice cream slowly.

He watched the water spraying from the beautiful Prometheus Fountain. He watched the droll penguins for a long time too.

But, besides Prometheus and the penguins, there were many other thoughts in Brian's head.

He was thinking of Mother and Happy-Go-

Lucky. He was thinking about Flora and wondering how long it would take a letter to travel from New York to Montreal.

Chapter Eight
Here Is Flora

It was most surprising, and it seemed too good to be true, but not two weeks after the British broadcast, here was Flora at Number Seven Hickory Drive. She had come to make a long visit too.

This is how it happened.

Brian had written to Flora the moment he had learned from Ben Bower her address in Montreal. Then, before his letter could have reached her, the postman handed Brian an envelope in Flora's handwriting. It was addressed to Brian in care of the New York Broadcasting Station, and down in one corner, Flora had written "Please Forward" with two lines drawn underneath.

It seems that Flora had been so excited when she heard Brian's voice on the air that she could hardly wait to write him. Flora wrote that she was living in Montreal with Auntie Grace and Uncle David Breen. Unlike Brian, Flora had traveled safely on a ship to Canada. Auntie Grace had met her at Quebec and taken her to Montreal. The journey had been as simple as could be.

Now that Brian and Flora could reach one another, letters began to fly back and forth between Hickory Drive and Victoria Avenue, Montreal. Uncle George laughed at Brian's ink-stained fingers and teased him about a spot of ink on his nose.

Then Aunt Jane and Auntie Grace wrote to one another, and one exciting day, an invitation was sent to Flora to come and pay Brian a visit.

Back came two answers at once.

Auntie Grace wrote that Flora might come. She was glad that Aunt Jane had said Flora might go to school with Brian. Auntie Grace thanked Aunt Jane for her invitation and hoped that Brian would visit them in Montreal before long.

Flora's letter was all excitement. It was mostly about times tables. Uncle David was helping her, she wrote.

So Flora arrived, looking just as Brian remembered, except that she was three inches taller.

Flora was sandy Scottish, with bright blue eyes and a freckle or two. The first thing you saw when she took off her hat was a big plaid hair ribbon. She was wearing her silver birthday bracelet too.

She and Brian were so glad to see one another that they went about smiling broadly. And how much they both did have to say!

"Tell me everything," said Flora.

When Brian had talked his throat dry so that he had to have a drink of water, then Flora took her turn. Aunt Jane smiled to herself as Flora's tongue tripped on and on.

She was a lively little girl. The very first evening, after dinner, Flora danced the Highland Fling. She made Brian dance too. Aunt Jane hunted up the music and played for them. Uncle George watched them over his evening paper.

"You are out of practice," Flora told Brian. "You must try to dance on just one spot. Do this step again."

Flora put Brian through his paces, over and over, until Aunt Jane suggested cookies and bed.

"That little girl has plenty of bounce," said Uncle George with a laugh as Flora and Brian disappeared upstairs.

Flora was a pleasant visitor. She fit in nicely and made herself useful whenever she could.

When she went marketing with Aunt Jane, she carried the bundles from the shop to the car.

She fed Victory and washed his saucer so nicely that Paula didn't mind having her in the kitchen at all. Indeed, Paula liked to talk to Flora. She told her all about her little girl, Stella.

Stella lived with her grandmother, her "babka," on the other side of the railroad tracks. Stella was to take part in a wedding shortly, Paula said. She was to wear a white dress and hold the bride's bouquet when the groom put the ring upon the finger of the bride.

Flora made friends all round about. The children at school liked her. Flora made them laugh, on purpose, when she talked about having "parritch" for breakfast. She taught them a guessing game, too, with strange, singsong words, "Nievie-nievie-nice-nack!" that rang in their heads.

Adam, in particular, liked Flora. He thought she was sensible, for she behaved well at his turtle, Poke's, funeral.

"Named Poke because he likes to be slow," explained Adam in a low voice.

There was no smiling or giggling on Flora's part. She knew that Adam felt truly sorry at his loss.

But, best of all, Flora didn't make fun of Adam's knitting. She looked soberly at the gray sock, which seemed to grow longer and thinner with every row, and in an instant told him how it might be put to use.

"If you make the other sock the regular size," said Flora, "they would do for a soldier with one injured leg, very thin, and one good one."

This was a splendid idea, and it cheered Adam immensely. He had spent many hours at work on that sock and didn't want to think his time wasted.

Van and Flora took to one another at once. This was just what Brian wanted. But Van would call Flora Miss McFlimsey.

"It is MacDonald, Van," Brian told him over and over. "Flora MacDonald."

But Van only laughed.

"'Miss Flora McFlimsey of Madison Square,'" was Van's answer. "Haven't you ever heard of her? She has trunks full of clothes, but 'I've heard her declare. . .Really and truly I've nothing to wear.'"

"That is not like me," said Flora stoutly. "I have plenty of clothes. You ought to see my MacDonald Clan tartan dress. And I wear a Scottish costume when I dance the Highland Fling."

"So you see, she can't be called Miss McFlimsey," said Brian, settling the question.

Every night before dinner, Flora heard Brian recite the Gettysburg Address. Mrs. King had given Brian more time in which to learn it. Flora would hold Victory on her lap as she drilled Brian from his *Token of Freedom*, and Victory would purr loudly as if he approved of every word.

"Tomorrow is the wedding," Flora told Brian one evening. "I am going with Paula to see Stella hold the bride's bouquet. Paula invited me, and Aunt Jane said I might go."

It was early the next afternoon that Paula and Flora started out. They were going first to Babka's house so that Paula might curl Stella's hair. Then they would all go to the wedding.

Stella was watching for them at the window. She was a shy little girl, about as old as Flora. She was excited, no wonder, and her eyes were bright, and her cheeks were very pink. She stood in her white petticoat before her mother while Paula brushed her soft yellow hair into stiff round curls.

Babka was bending over the ironing board, pressing Stella's white dress.

"It was a little creased from hanging in the closet," explained Babka. "There should not be one wrinkle when Stella stands up with the bride to hold her bouquet."

Babka pressed slowly. She was taking great pains.

The curls were finished now. Stella was waiting to have the white dress slipped over her head.

Suddenly Babka cried aloud.

"Oh! Oh!" she moaned, and set down her iron with a thump.

She sank into a chair and covered her face with her hands.

"Are you hurt?" cried Paula. "Have you pain? Speak! Tell me."

Stella was frightened. She pulled at her grandmother's apron and called, "Babka! Babka!"

Flora stood staring. She didn't know what to do.

By this time Babka was feebly shaking her head.

"It is ruined," she whispered. "I have ruined Stella's dress."

Paula and Stella and Flora crowded round the ironing board to look.

The skirt of the dress was scorched a deep dark yellow. The spot was directly in front. It couldn't be hidden. How such a thing had happened no one could say, poor Babka least of all.

Babka was crying. Stella was crying too. Paula, with a sober face, was trying to wash out the spot.

"The spot is there to stay," said Paula at last, "and it is as large as a man's straw hat. The dress cannot be worn."

At this dreadful news, Stella's sobs grew loud.

"The wedding! The wedding!" she cried. "What shall I wear?"

The clock was ticking away the moments. The hands seemed to move very fast.

A thought came to Flora.

Quickly she unbuttoned her coat.

"Here," said Flora. "Wear my dress."

Flora's dress was white with a tiny blue flower. There was lace about the neck and on the sleeves. It would do nicely for the wedding if only it would fit.

For a moment Paula looked doubtful. Then she changed her mind.

She helped Flora out of the dress. She slipped it over Stella's head.

"It fits! It fits!" cried Flora, clapping her hands.

So it did, well enough. Paula turned Stella round and round and slowly nodded her head.

"It will do," said Paula. "It is a little large, but it will do. See, Babka. Our Stella looks well. No more tears, Stella. You have a beautiful dress to wear."

Struck with a thought, Paula turned to Flora.

"But what," asked Paula, "will you wear?"

"My coat," answered Flora, pulling it on and buttoning it tight. "My petticoat will look like the white dress underneath."

And that was the way they went to the wedding.

"I had a good time," said Flora that evening. "The bride was beautiful, and Stella looked lovely too. She took the bouquet and held it just right. Such good things to eat afterward! Babka saw that I had all the cake I wanted. It tasted like rich raisin bread. And Babka kissed me when I came away."

At this moment, Van put his head in at the door. He and Uncle George were going to a meeting together.

"Oh, Miss McFlimsey," said Van, raising his eyebrows at Flora. "Brian tells me you went to a wedding today and 'really and truly had nothing to wear.'"

"No, I didn't," answered Flora with spirit. "I wore my blue coat. Nobody at the wedding knew I didn't have a dress on, and most of the time I forgot it myself."

Chapter Nine
The British Benefit

Everyone on Hickory Drive was working for the British Benefit. Everyone, that is, except Van, who had gone away on a lecture trip.

The money was going toward a British-American Ambulance to be sent to England. On the afternoon of the Benefit, the Thumbs Up Shop, where the Benefit was held, was crowded to the doors.

People had given articles to be placed on sale, something that came from England or Scotland or

Wales. Sometimes they were just things that people had at home and didn't want any longer. But the Odds and Ends table was such a success that, before the day was over, everything was sold.

Refreshments might be bought too. Auntie Grace in Montreal had sent her Scottish recipe for scones. Any number of them had been baked by Paula to be sold with tea or by the dozen. Flora, wearing a Scotch plaid gingham dress, helped both to serve and to sell.

Brian was there with Victory. The head of the Benefit had especially wanted Victory to come.

"Two little English refugees," people said when they saw them together.

They stroked and patted Victory, who took it nicely and seemed to enjoy the attention. But it made Brian feel homesick to be called a refugee.

Aunt Jane seemed to understand how Brian was feeling. Perhaps she could see it in his face.

"Don't mind them," she whispered. "You are not a refugee. You are part of the family."

That made Brian feel cheerful again.

A pretty young lady from Wales named Gweneth Lloyd-Jones, sang "There'll Always Be an England" and "Men of Harlech." When she was not singing, she sat at the piano and softly played old Scotch and English airs.

All sorts of people came and looked about and had tea and scones or tea and English muffins. They bought things, and they let Aunt Jane show them all the knitted garments they had made themselves and that were to be sent to England.

Adam's mother was serving tea, and Adam himself was there, doing a rushing business. For Adam was managing a Grab Bag, and the Grab Bag was the long thin sock.

In the beginning, Adam had wanted to show his knitting at the Benefit like everyone else. But so far he had made only one sock. He hadn't even started the other one yet. The more he thought of it, the more he felt it would be hard to find a British soldier who could wear the sock. So the idea came to him of turning the sock into a Grab Bag.

Adam's father liked the idea. He said he believed that a Grab Bag would do more for the British Army than the sock. He gave Adam a dollar, and Adam spent a happy afternoon at the Five and Ten Cent Store choosing articles that would be slim enough to fit into the sock.

He bought wisely, and he wrapped each purchase in white paper tied with red, white, and blue cord.

He told Brian and Flora exactly what he had bought, and they agreed that people couldn't help being pleased, no matter what they pulled from the Bag. Adam bought an egg cup to fill the foot, and the long leg was packed with a paper of pins, two pencils, a thimble, three hatpins, a ruby ring, two spools of thread, a necktie, two kitchen spoons, a pair of green earrings, three lollipops, a screwdriver, and a box of nails.

Adam had made a large sign. It read:

V for Victory Grab Bag

Don't fail to miss it

V cents a Grab

Adam was puzzled to know why the sign made everyone laugh. But if they came to laugh, they stayed to buy, and soon the Grab Bag was empty, and Adam's money box was full.

The afternoon was going well. Scones and muffins were vanishing. Vases, picture frames, sprays of pressed heather, Toby jugs, and paper weights were selling fast.

Gweneth Lloyd-Jones had just finished singing "Flow Gently, Sweet Afton" when Mrs. Van Rensselaer Green walked into the room.

Mrs. Van Rensselaer Green was a kindly, stout, red-faced woman. People liked her. She was wealthy, and she was both generous and good-hearted in the use of her money.

Now she walked about the room, buying of everyone. To Adam's surprise, she bought his sock that lay empty on a table under the sign.

"I have a very good use for that," she said. She pressed a quarter into Adam's hand.

Everyone wondered what she would do with the sock, but no one liked to ask.

Mrs. Green might have told them that she intended to give it to her maid to polish silver. But she didn't say. And it is just as well for Adam, for he thought she meant to wear it as a scarf.

Now Mrs. Green spied Victory in Brian's arms.

"A British refugee kitten!" exclaimed Mrs. Green when she heard Victory's story. "Oh, I must have him. I know a little English boy in New York who is very homesick. He adores cats, and I am sure he would be happy and contented if he could own this kitten. It is for sale, is it not?"

"I—I hadn't thought of selling him," faltered Brian. He was confused about what to do.

He tightened his hold on Victory as he spoke.

"Oh, but you must!" cried Mrs. Green. "When I think of little Michael so lonely without his mother, I know what this kitten would mean to him. I will give fifty dollars for him. Think how that would help the Ambulance Fund!"

Fifty dollars! Brian was surprised.

It seemed a great deal of money to Brian. But part with Victory—how could he?

Brian didn't know what he ought to do. Mrs. Green was waiting for his answer. Other people were looking on and waiting too.

Adam tried to help Brian. He shook his head violently and whispered in Brian's ear.

"Keep your cat," he said.

Brian looked at Aunt Jane.

"You must make up your own mind, Brian," said Aunt Jane gently. "But remember how much you love Victory."

If Aunt Jane hadn't said the word "remember" perhaps Brian would have acted differently. But "remember" was the word Mother had used.

"Remember, Uphold England," she had said.

Twice she had spoken those very words. Once was when they said goodbye at the port in England. The other time was on the broadcast when her voice had sounded so natural and so near.

Brian was thinking very fast.

If he should let Victory go, what a fine way to Uphold England! There would be fifty dollars more for the British-American Ambulance Fund, and a little homesick English boy would be made happy with an English pet.

Brian looked down at Victory. The kitten was purring softly. Slowly he closed his eyes in content.

"I don't believe he will be homesick," thought Brian. "He didn't seem to miss his mother when Lady Diana gave him to me."

This was very true. How comfortably Victory had settled himself in bed with Brian their very first night in the United States and had gone straight to sleep without any fuss.

Uphold England!

No one said it, but the words sounded plainly in Brian's ears.

He made up his mind.

Quickly he lifted Victory and let Mrs. Green take him in her arms.

"I will sell him for England," said Brian. "But tell Michael to let Victory sleep with him the very first night."

Mrs. Green acted quickly too. She counted out five new ten-dollar bills.

"They are yours, to give to England," she said.

That is what Brian did. The head of the Benefit stood beside him, and Brian put the money into her hand.

Then, with Victory clinging to her shoulder, Mrs. Green was gone. Brian was glad that Victory didn't look frightened as he went out of the door.

Adam knew how his friend was feeling. He missed his turtle, Poke, and how much more would Brian miss his lively kitten.

"You did a lot for England today," said Adam.

"I am going to write to your mother tonight," said Aunt Jane on the way home. "She will be proud of what you have done. Your father must know it too."

All this was pleasant and comforting.

Flora was kind and thoughtful too. The moment she was in the house, Flora hurried Victory's basket into the attic out of sight.

"Brian won't want to see it standing around empty," she explained in a whisper to Aunt Jane.

After dinner, Flora suggested that they practice the Highland Fling.

"We must be careful about our gestures," said Flora. "Arms over head. Now, hands on hips."

They stopped for a moment to catch their breath.

"I have had an idea come to me," said Flora. "It is a secret yet, but pretty soon I can tell."

This was mysterious. It made Brian forget Victory and set him to wondering what the secret might be.

"Promise to tell me first," said Brian.

"I will," answered Flora with a laugh. "You will be the very first one to know."

Chapter Ten
In Place of Victory

The next morning the doorbell rang early.

"Tweet-tweet-tweet! Twee-twee-twee-tweet!" floated into the house when Paula opened the door. It was a high, shrill, piercing song.

In a few moments, the door shut and Paula came into the dining room where they all sat at breakfast. She was carrying a large gilt cage, and in the cage was a bright-eyed yellow canary. The canary was singing.

He kept right on singing when Paula set the cage on the breakfast table near Brian's place.

"It was Mrs. Van Rensselaer Green's chauffeur at the door," announced Paula, "and he brought this bird as a present for Brian. It is to take the place of the kitten, Mrs. Green sent word. It isn't from her exactly. It is from the lady who lives next door to her. But the lady heard from Mrs. Green about Brian selling Victory for England, and so she wanted to give him her bird."

Brian was pleased at having a present. He and Flora stood up to look at the canary. The bird was a colorful little fellow with shining black eyes.

"That was very kind of Mrs. Green's neighbor," began Aunt Jane. "Didn't you learn her name, Paula? Brian must write her a letter of thanks."

Aunt Jane's voice grew louder and louder as she spoke. This was because she wanted to be heard, and the canary was still singing. He had never stopped.

"The lady doesn't want to be thanked," called

back Paula. "She is going away today for the summer, and her house will be closed."

"Oh!" said Aunt Jane. "Well, Paula, take the bird upstairs, please. He will quiet down when his cage is hung."

"Yes, Mrs. Bliss," answered Paula loudly. "There is a big stand in the hall to hold the cage."

"I'll carry the stand upstairs," said Brian.

"I can help," offered Flora.

Paula still stood in the doorway.

"The bird's name is Tweetie," she called.

Her voice was almost a shriek.

"Twee-twee-tweet," wafted downstairs as Tweetie, singing cheerily, was carried up. His tall gilt stand followed, with Brian and Flora at either end.

"Quite a racket," said Uncle George mildly. "Tweetie seems to have good lungs."

"Yes, hasn't he?" agreed Aunt Jane, drawing a long breath. "But it only needs a dark cloth over a cage to keep a bird quiet, you know."

It was too bad Brian had to go to school that

morning. Only Flora and Paula were at home when the rabbits and the turtle arrived.

They didn't come together.

The two rabbits came in a crate. The Expressman brought them.

A card was tacked on the crate. "The Sunshine Club sends these pets to the little English boy who gave his kitten for England," it read.

Paula told the Expressman to set the crate in the back garden. She and Flora were looking at the rabbits when a small thin man came walking around the side of the house.

It was Professor Capes, who lived around the corner on Mountain Avenue. He was a scientist who spent his days working in a brick laboratory behind his house.

Professor Capes carried a bag, and from it he took a turtle. The turtle, during his journey, had drawn himself inside his shell. But, placed on the grass, out came his head and tail and four feet and off he started toward the lilac bush.

"I brought this turtle for Brian Blythe," said the Professor. "I have no further use for it in my research work, and I happened to be drinking tea at the Benefit yesterday when he parted with his kitten. Remembering my own boyhood, I thought he might like this new pet."

Paula said nothing. She was looking at the turtle as if she didn't like him very well.

So Flora answered.

"Thank you," said Flora politely. "Brian will like the turtle."

She was thinking of Adam and how fond he had been of Poke.

The Professor bowed to Flora. He acted as if she were grown-up.

"Will you tell Brian," went on Professor Capes, "that this turtle was given me by a full-blooded American Indian? It makes it more interesting, I think."

"Yes, I will," promised Flora as the Professor walked quietly away.

She gazed at the turtle with new respect.

But Paula felt differently.

"American Indian or not," said Paula, "what are we to do with a turtle underfoot? But it is a mercy that the gentleman didn't bring something worse. I have heard he has monkeys and snakes and whatnot shut up in that strange little work-house of his."

When Aunt Jane came home, she looked at the rabbits and the turtle without saying a single word. Even down in the garden, they could hear Tweetie singing. His cage was covered with Aunt Jane's old black silk skirt. But he was singing as happily as if he were out in the sunshine.

"Well," said Aunt Jane at last, "I only hope these pets make Brian happy."

Brian was excited about the rabbits when he came home at noon. He liked the turtle, too, and named him Poke the Second.

"That will please Adam," he said.

That afternoon Brian and Patsy built a rabbit hutch of packing boxes. Patsy was the man who cut the grass for the Blisses. His real name was Pasquale, but he liked to be called Patsy instead.

It was fun to watch the ruby eyes and twitching noses of the two rabbits who lived in the hutch. Uncle George named one of them Wigglesworth, because of his nose, and Flora wanted to call the other one Snowflake. Wigglesworth and Snowflake liked cabbage and lettuce. They ate a great deal. It kept Brian and Flora busy, poking cabbage and lettuce leaves into the hutch.

Unlike Tweetie, the rabbits were quiet. But though their hutch was well built and comfortable, they didn't like to stay at home. In some way they managed to squeeze themselves out and always at an inconvenient time.

"The rabbits are out," Paula would call.

Then, no matter what Brian and Flora were doing, they would have to chase the rabbits all over the garden and drive them home.

"The turtle is the best of the lot," said Adam.

But Paula wouldn't agree. The turtle liked to climb out of his box and wander across the kitchen floor. Of course he got in Paula's way. And every time she stepped on him, it startled her, and she screamed.

Brian began to feel that his new pets were not much fun. They were no comfort at all. He never let himself think about Victory if he could help it. Not one of these pets could compare with Victory in any way.

On Paula's night out, Uncle George said he would take the family off somewhere to dinner. They all wanted to get away from Tweetie's singing and from chasing rabbits and hearing Paula step on Poke.

So they went, and they had a good time, with a long drive into the country to give them a change of scenery.

It was pleasant, too, to reach home and find Tweetie sound asleep with his head under his wing. The rabbits were safe in their hutch. Brian ran out with a flashlight to look. Only the turtle was not where he should be. He had crawled off and hidden himself and couldn't be found.

But the next morning the house was upset again.

It was Saturday. Tweetie began the day by singing in a hearty voice the moment the sun was up. He woke everyone an hour too soon.

Then Paula had no sooner creaked downstairs than Brian and Flora heard the familiar call.

"The rabbits are out! Hurry! The rabbits are out!" Paula cried.

It was too early to hurry. But Paula didn't stop calling for Brian and Flora.

"They are over in Mr. Van's garden," cried Paula. "Logan said he would make them into rabbit stew if he caught them at his vegetables again."

This was a horrible thought. Brian and Flora didn't stop to dress. They ran over the grass in their pajamas. But here was Logan, bringing the rabbits back himself.

He carried them by the ears, and the rabbits looked very miserable. But at least they were not being made into stew.

Logan seemed to know what the children were thinking.

"Next time—" said Logan.

That was all. But they knew very well what he meant.

Aunt Jane looked white at breakfast. Her head ached a little, she said.

"Your uncle has shut Tweetie in the guest room," she said, "and my head will be better soon."

Uncle George was late this morning, and the train was always on time. He finished his breakfast quickly. He stood up and took one step. Then he tripped over something that sent him stumbling across the room.

"Jehoshaphat!" exclaimed Uncle George as he was caught by surprise.

He caught hold of the lowboy just in time to save himself from a fall.

Of course it was the fault of Poke the Second. He must have been hiding under the table and came walking out at just the wrong time. He didn't seem to mind being stepped on. He went crawling off toward the kitchen as calm as you please.

Uncle George put on his hat.

"This house isn't fit to live in," he said.

Then he hurried off without a goodbye. He really didn't have a minute. They all could hear the whistle of his train.

Brian and Flora went out to feed Wigglesworth and Snowflake. But even the hutch full of greens didn't keep them at home.

"The rabbits are out," Paula kept calling.

They had to be chased twice.

Then Professor Capes came to call. He brought with him a monkey-cat for Brian.

The monkey-cat was part cat and part monkey, the Professor told them. But Brian thought it looked more like a cat.

Aunt Jane was polite but very firm.

"We couldn't possibly have another animal in this house, Professor Capes," said she.

"I see, I see," said the Professor gently.

And he went away, but not before the monkey-cat had jumped from the Professor's arms, climbed the curtain, and sat above the window, chattering at them all. The Professor had to coax and coax before it would come down.

"A monkey-cat is very strange," said Flora when they were alone.

"I feel strange, too," said Brian. "Don't you think we have chased these rabbits a hundred miles?"

Tweetie was singing away in the guest room, and Aunt Jane lay down on her bed with a wet towel over her forehead.

Paula was banging pots and pans in the kitchen. She sounded upset.

Indeed, Paula was so upset that at luncheon she came walking into the dining room. You could see there was something she wanted to say.

"The rabbits are out," said Paula, "and I have just stepped on the turtle again. I am leaving, Mrs. Bliss, as soon as you can be suited with somebody else. I can do the work of a house, but I won't live in a zoo."

For a moment no one moved or spoke.

Brian and Flora didn't run after the rabbits. They were tired.

Aunt Jane didn't answer Paula. Instead she put her hands to her head.

"This doesn't seem like home any more," said Aunt Jane slowly.

Then, without another word, she walked off and went upstairs.

Flora looked frightened, but Brian felt brave.

"Something will have to be done about this," said Brian. "Come on, Flora. Let's think what to do."

Chapter Eleven
What They Did

Paula went into the kitchen and began to wash the dishes. She didn't bang a single pot or pan.

Brian caught Poke the Second and put him in his box. He tied a string around the box as you would a parcel, only there was no cover. Now Poke couldn't climb out.

"Paula won't step on Poke ever again," said Brian firmly. "Do you know why? Because we are going to give him to Adam. Adam isn't home now, but he will be before long."

"That's a good idea!" cried Flora. "Won't Adam be glad! Brian, why can't we give all the animals away?"

"We can," answered Brian boldly, "and we will as soon as we find out where to give them to."

"We ought to get rid of Tweetie first," suggested Flora, "because he is making Aunt Jane's head ache. Do we dare give him away with that lovely cage and stand? What do you suppose Mrs. Green would say?"

"He wasn't Mrs. Green's bird," said Brian. "Anyway, he is my bird now. Of course Tweetie and the cage and the stand all go together. But where will they go?"

Flora wrinkled up her forehead. She was thinking hard.

"I know," she said suddenly. "Miss Birch would like a bird. She lives all alone in that great big house, and she looks out of the window for company. She told Aunt Jane that she did."

"So she does," agreed Brian. "That was how she saw me lose my snake belt."

"Miss Birch doesn't hear so well," went on Flora. "She wouldn't mind how much Tweetie sings."

"We will go ask her right this minute if she wouldn't like a bird." said Brian. "I do hope she is home."

Miss Birch was at home. Her little round apple face creased with smiles when she heard about the canary.

It was just as Flora thought.

"I should like him for company," said Miss Birch at once. "His singing wouldn't bother me. I'd enjoy it. I don't hear quite so well as I did when I was young. But are you sure your Aunt Jane will be willing to part with him?"

"Yes, I am sure," answered Brian. "He has a cage and stand. May we bring him here now?"

"Yes, indeed," said Miss Birch happily. "I will make a place for his cage in front of this window. He can look out of one window, and I shall look out of the other."

Paula helped in the moving. She carried Tweetie in the cage. Brian and Flora managed the stand.

"Be as quiet as you can," said Paula. "Your poor Aunt Jane has fallen asleep."

They made a funny procession, marching down the street to the tune of Tweetie's music. But they were met with smiles by Miss Birch in her doorway. The stand was set in the window and the cage hung in place.

"Thank you over and over," said little Miss Birch. "Tweetie and I are going to be happy here together."

It really seemed so as they left Tweetie singing to Miss Birch, each in a window looking out upon the street.

It was on the way home that Flora stopped short and gave a shriek.

"The rabbits!" she cried. "We forgot the rabbits. Suppose they are in Van's garden! What if Logan has made them into a stew?"

The best way to find out was to go and see Logan.

Patsy was cutting Van's lawn, and Logan sat at work on the back steps. Logan wore an apron made of bedticking and he was busily polishing brasses. He didn't look as if he had been cooking rabbit stew.

"Mr. Van is coming home next week," said Logan. "Go look in the hutch for your rabbits. I put them there an hour ago."

"Oh, Logan, how good you are!" cried Flora. "I knew you wouldn't do anything so mean."

"I wasn't hungry," answered Logan with a grin. "How are you getting on with your menagerie next door?"

Brian told of the day's doing. Patsy stopped work and came to listen too.

"We have given Tweetie to Miss Birch," said Brian. "Now we want to find a home for the rabbits. Wouldn't you like them, Patsy? Haven't you any children who would like a pair of nice white rabbits?"

"Not me," answered Patsy, with a shrug. "Give the rabbits to the Italian Orphanage. Lots of little boys and girls with no mamma and no papa. The

Sisters mind them. Ask Sister Angelina to take the rabbits. She likes nice things."

"You ask her, Patsy," begged Brian. "Telephone and ask if she will take our rabbits. We do want to give them away."

Patsy was obliging. He smiled and showed his white teeth and went into the house to telephone.

Logan rubbed away at his brasses.

"How will the Sunshine Club like it when they hear what you have done with their present?" he asked.

"I don't know anybody in the Sunshine Club," answered Brian, "and they don't know me. They didn't ask whether I liked rabbits. Rabbits are not like Victory, not one bit."

Flora had followed Patsy into the house, and now she came running back.

Brian could tell from her face that she had good news.

"Yes, yes!" cried Flora. "She will! She will!"

"Sister Angelina is a good woman," said Patsy, close behind. "She says, 'Yes, bring the rabbits.'"

"How?" asked Brian. "How can we carry them there? The Orphanage is way out on the River Road."

"My friend Dominick is coming by for me in his truck," said Patsy. "He will take the rabbits. Maybe take you too."

Dominick was good-natured. He and Patsy carried the rabbit hutch to the truck. Patsy lifted Flora to the seat beside Dominick, and he and Brian sat at the tail of the truck with their feet swinging. Brian held on tight as he bumped along, but he thought it was fun.

The Italian Orphanage was a red-brick building standing under tall trees.

Sister Angelina came out to meet them. She showed Patsy and Dominick where to place the rabbit hutch. Then she turned toward the house and beckoned.

The children must have been waiting for this signal, for out of the house they ran. There were twenty little boys and girls, most of them with dark hair and large dark eyes.

They were delighted with the rabbits. They danced about the hutch and laughed with pleasure. They asked more questions than anyone could answer, even Sister Angelina. A few of them patted the rabbits gently and stroked the soft white fur.

Flora made friends with the little girls. Josephine, Annunziata, Elena, and Concetta crowded around her. Little Elena seized Flora's hand and kissed it.

Brian showed Tony and Joey and Benito how to feed the rabbits with the cabbage and carrots left in the hutch.

Then it was time to go. Flora curtsied goodbye to gentle Sister Angelina, and Brian made his politest bow.

"Good work," said Brian, as they rolled home. "They are all gone now but Poke the Second."

"And Adam has come home," added Flora, when they reached Hickory Drive. "He is out on his steps."

"I wish I hadn't missed it all," said Adam with regret, as he heard how the afternoon had been spent. "I will take Poke the Second."

It was almost time for dinner. Aunt Jane sat in the living room. Her headache was gone, and she was wearing her prettiest dress. Uncle George was home too. He had brought Aunt Jane a box of candy. Paula was quietly lighting the tall pink candles in the dining room.

"I was so surprised," said Aunt Jane, "when I woke up and found the pets gone. But it is just as well, I think. They will be happy in their new homes."

"A fine afternoon's work," said Uncle George. "I am delighted."

He laughed and patted Brian on the back. And everyone else laughed too.

Dinner was ready.

As Paula went to and fro, her face wore a triumphant look. It was not only that Poke was gone from under her feet. It was because Paula had a surprise waiting.

The surprise was fresh strawberry ice cream for dessert. Paula had thought of it all by herself.

"It is a celebration," said Paula.

And they all knew what she meant.

"This never happened at Happy-Go-Lucky,"

thought Brian. "It's easy to have ice cream in America. I wish Mother was here."

"Doesn't this seem like home again?" asked Aunt Jane, when the ice cream had disappeared.

Uncle George nodded as he lighted his cigar.

"Not one of those animals was anything like Victory," began Brian.

"I should think not," answered Flora quickly.

But she had something else in mind.

"Brian, do you remember that I said I had a secret?" she asked. "Well, I ought to have a letter from Auntie Grace on Monday and, if I do, then I can tell."

Chapter Twelve
Flora's Secret

Flora's letter from Auntie Grace arrived on Monday morning.

Soon thereafter, the Expressman left a big box at the door. Flora could hardly wait for Brian to come home from school.

"Open it! Open it!" cried Flora before he was fairly in the house. "It is the secret, and you must open the box."

Aunt Jane and Paula stood by to watch.

Brian cut the string. Off came the cover.

There lay Flora's Scottish costume in which she danced the Highland Fling.

Out came the plaid kilt, the pretty white ruffled blouse, and the black velvet jacket. Out came the bonnet with a feather, and shoes with silver buckles, and a pair of tartan hose.

"There is my sporran!" cried Flora.

She was so excited that she could hardly stand still.

The sporran was a large pouch, covered with hair, and trimmed with two long black tassels. It fastened in front of the kilt at Flora's waist.

"The sporran is a purse," explained Flora. "It is part of the Highland costume. The Scottish regiments wear them. They look fine too."

"I have seen the Black Watch on parade," said Brian. "Father took me. I thought they were splendid. Is this the secret, Flora?"

Flora laughed and shook her head.

"Look in the box again," said she. "You haven't found the secret yet."

Brian hunted under the papers and brought out another sporran. He pulled out another kilt, a pair of plaid hose, and a bonnet.

Brian looked at Flora. What did this mean?

"It is the secret," cried Flora. "Now I can tell. I wanted you to have a costume like mine when we dance together. So Auntie Grace has sent these to you. They belonged to her friend's son, Robert Murray. But he is grown-up and can't wear them any longer, and so he has given them to you."

"To me?" asked Brian in surprise. "Are they really mine, for keeps?"

"They are yours, for keeps," answered Flora. "Auntie Grace said so in her letter this morning. Now you need only the blouse and the jacket and the shoes. But you really ought to wear white gaiters too, if you want to be just right."

"Oh, he must be right," Aunt Jane was saying. "My dressmaker will make the blouse and the jacket. The shoes won't be hard to find, and we can buy the gaiters in New York."

Brian's face was beaming. In this outfit he would look like a soldier of the Black Watch. He wished Mother could be here to see him, and Father too.

"If they could only walk over the Rainbow Bridge," thought Brian, "wouldn't it be just great?"

Flora was delighted that her plan was going so well.

"Won't it be fun to wear the costumes?" asked Flora. "Don't you like my secret?"

"Yes, I do," answered Brian truly.

"So do I," said Aunt Jane. "And I think you two ought to dance the Highland Fling at the entertainment the last day of school."

That was an idea!

"Wouldn't the boys stare?" began Brian. "But I am going to recite the Gettysburg Address, you know. Could I do both?"

"I don't know why not," was Aunt Jane's answer. "But we will see what Doctor Flower has to say."

Aunt Jane was pleased that Brian had left his shyness behind him. He no longer dreaded standing up and reciting before the school. And now he was more than willing; he was even eager to dance.

There was no reason why Brian shouldn't both recite and dance at the entertainment. Doctor Flower and Mrs. King liked the idea of the Scottish dance, and they made the Highland Fling the last number on the program.

"That is so the entertainment will close with something lively and stirring," said Mrs. King.

The busy days slipped by. Brian's costume was now ready. The white gaiters had been bought. The fine white blouse and velvet jacket hung in the closet. On the closet floor stood a pair of shoes with silver buckles. The Highland costume was complete.

Van came home the day before the entertainment. His lecture trip had been a great success.

Brian and Flora ran over to see him. They peered in at the French window, and Van spied them.

"Reel of cotton," called Brian quickly.

"Spool of thread," answered Van at once.

That was their greeting. They were still playing the game of words.

"Biscuits," ventured Flora.

"Crackers," said Van. "Come in, and tell me all the news."

Flora said at once, "Tell Van about Victory."

So Brian, with help from Flora, told.

"Brian gave Victory for England," insisted Flora. "Of course, he earned fifty dollars for the Ambulance Fund. But it was because of England that he let Victory go."

"I understand," said Van quietly. "That was a fine thing to do, old chap."

This praise made Brian happy. He went on to tell that he was to recite the Gettysburg Address at the entertainment the next day.

Van looked pleased when he heard this.

Flora couldn't wait any longer to tell her secret and how well it had turned out.

"We are going to end the program with our dance," said Flora proudly. "We know the steps perfectly, and our costumes are just right."

"Then you are not Miss McFlimsey this time, are you?" said Van, with a twinkle in his eye.

"No, nor ever was," answered Flora so promptly that it made both Van and Brian laugh.

Van laughed again over the household of pets that had proved so upsetting.

"Not one of them could take Victory's place," said Brian, "nor anywhere near it."

"Of course not," agreed Van. "It would have to be something very special to do that."

When the children left, Van went with them as far as his garage.

"I have an unexpected errand in New York," said Van. "It is something important that must be attended to at once."

He waved as he passed them on the driveway.

"See you tomorrow," called Van, "at the entertainment. I shall be there."

He left the children looking at one another in surprise.

So Van was coming to the entertainment.

"Won't I do my best tomorrow?" thought Brian. "Next to Mother and Father, I'd rather have Van come than anyone else."

"We mustn't make a single mistake in the dance," Flora was thinking.

She went through the opening steps on her toes in the grass.

Aunt Jane was surprised, too, when they told her.

"I didn't know Van could give the time," said Aunt Jane. "He is a very busy man."

"I never dreamed of Van's coming," said Brian. "We didn't ask him. He thought of it himself."

"He is coming to hear the Gettysburg Address," said Flora, "and perhaps he would like to see us in costume in the Highland Fling too."

Chapter Thirteen
The Last Day of School

The assembly room was crowded the next morning. Every child was in his place. Parents and friends had come to see the entertainment too. Aunt Jane sat in the very front row. A seat beside her had been saved for Van. On the other side of Aunt Jane sat Flora in her Scottish costume. Brian was to be helped into his suit by Mrs. King when his recitation was over.

Adam's mother sat near at hand. Adam was

to appear in a play called "John Smith and Pocahontas."

It was almost time for the entertainment to begin. Up the aisle walked Van. He was carrying a wicker basket. He sat down beside Aunt Jane. He set the basket at his feet.

This seemed odd to Brian. He longed to know what was in the basket. Flora was leaning forward, peering down at Van's feet. She was curious too. Neither of them guessed that here was the reason for Van's sudden trip, yesterday, into New York.

Adam's play came quite soon in the program. Adam took the part of John Smith. Barbara Novak made a sturdy, pleasing Pocahontas. Walter Collins and Charles Robinson and Stanley Koshenski were the Indians who would have killed John Smith if Pocahontas had not saved him.

It was an exciting play, with scenery and costumes made by the actors. They had written the play too. One of the actors was missing, though the audience did not know it. It was Poke the

Second. That very morning he had wandered off and couldn't be found. John Smith and the Indians were keenly disappointed. But Pocahontas was happy, for Poke would creep under her feet and had made her tumble once or twice.

Everyone seemed to enjoy the play. Brian and Flora and Van and Aunt Jane and Adam's mother clapped the loudest of all.

The entertainment moved along quickly. Now it was Brian's turn to recite.

"'Fourscore and seven years ago,'" he began.

At first, when he looked down from the platform, he saw only row after row of strange faces. But this lasted only a moment. Brian's voice grew steady. He felt sure of himself.

"'. . . a new nation, conceived in liberty, and dedicated to the proposition that all men are created equal,'" he was saying.

Now he could pick out Van's face and Aunt Jane's and Flora's. He saw that they all looked very proud. Brian thought they were proud of the fine words he was reciting. So they were. But they were proud, too, that Brian was speaking so clearly and easily and so well.

"'. . . that this nation, under God, shall have a new birth of freedom; and that government of the people, by the people, for the people, shall not perish from the Earth.'"

That was the end.

After Brian's recitation, Doctor Flower gave out prizes. They were for scholarship and good attendance. Four boys and girls filed up to receive them. In every case the prize was a book.

When that was over, Doctor Flower looked straight down at Van and nodded.

To everyone's surprise, Van, with his basket, mounted the platform.

Van was used to an audience. He knew just how to speak.

"I want to tell you a story," he began.

Very simply, Van told the story of a boy and his kitten, and it was about Brian and Victory.

"This boy," said Van, "sold his British refugee kitten to Uphold England. He gave the money to the British-American Ambulance Fund. Most of you know that the boy is Brian Blythe. I want Brian to come up on the platform to receive, not a prize, because you don't win a prize for loving your country, but a present."

Brian walked up on the platform. It was all so easy and natural that Brian didn't remember that he was on a platform at all. It was just as if he were talking to Van at home.

"This is a present," said Van to Brian, "given to show American friendship for a British guest."

Van opened the basket. He took out a jet-black kitten. He held the kitten so that everyone in the room could see.

"This is your kitten, Brian," said Van. "He is an American kitten, and his name is Liberty."

Brian held out his arms, and Liberty snuggled down in them exactly as Victory had done. How good it felt to hold a warm, furry kitten again!

Liberty's little pointed face was bright and

spirited. He had topaz eyes, and his nose was very pink. Brian knew the moment he saw Liberty that they were going to be good friends.

"Thank you, Van," said Brian, hugging Liberty close. "Thank you very much."

Liberty looked out at the audience. He gave his head a shake, and then he sneezed. It was a funny little cat sneeze. It made everyone in the Assembly Room laugh. It gave the children a chance to clap their hands. All the grown people, who had been feeling proud of Brian, were glad to clap too. The funny sneeze was the best thing Liberty could have done. He couldn't have thought of anything better if he had tried.

Brian walked down from the platform. He would have whistled a little tune if he hadn't been at the entertainment. He was so happy that for the moment he forgot the Highland Fling. But Mrs. King had not forgotten. She was beckoning Brian to hurry. So Van took Liberty, and Brian ran off to change into his costume. He and Mrs. King worked so quickly that he was dressed and waiting before the school had finished the song they were singing.

Now for the Highland Fling.

Brian and Flora took their places. Mrs. King was seated at the piano, and the dance began.

They danced on one small spot. Their nimble feet twinkled to and fro. They went through every graceful gesture. Flora had drilled Brian well. Their bright tartan kilts swung in time to the music. The silver shoe buckles flashed. Their bonnets were set at a jaunty tilt.

It was a lively, merry dance. It seemed as if they would never tire. Flora was happy and smiling. Brian was smiling too.

Brian and Flora had never danced so well. But, after all, how could they help it? For there they were, dancing in the midst of friends, while Liberty looked on with shining eyes.